"Oh!" Laura put a ha[...] throat. She'd expected to see Guy in a seersucker or linen suit to help him endure the summer heat.

He turned from the mirror. "You don't approve?"

"Oh, I approve. I'm just surprised at your choice." A cobalt-blue Western-cut shirt that matched his beautiful eyes stretched across his broad shoulders. Dark denim jeans cinched with a black belt led down to square-toed black boots. The transformation from stuffy businessman to cowboy suited him. "You look very handsome."

The happiness dancing in Guy's eyes at her compliment pulled instant heat to her cheeks and widened her smile.

Their gazes locked. She delighted in the appreciation shining from Guy's eyes, yet she knew it wasn't proper to allow a man to look at her in this way in a public place, especially with a salesclerk and Clifford looking on.

Books by Rose Ross Zediker

Love Inspired Heartsong Presents

Wedding on the Rocks
The Widow's Suitor
Sweet on the Cowgirl

ROSE ROSS ZEDIKER

started her writing career in 1991, focusing on children's writing. She found success penning short stories, nonfiction and devotions for Sunday school take-home papers, tallying sixty-plus bylines. She started writing inspirational romance novels in 2009 and saw her first book published in 2010.

Rose and her husband live in rural southeastern South Dakota. Her son and daughter-in-law blessed them with two beautiful granddaughters. Rose spends her days working at the University of South Dakota and writes during her evenings and weekends. She balances both careers with relaxing hobbies: sewing, embroidery, quilting, reading and spoiling her granddaughters.

Please visit her on the web
at www.roserosszediker.blogspot.com
or at her group blog, www.inkspirationalmessages.com.

ROSE ROSS ZEDIKER

Sweet on the Cowgirl

HEARTSONG
PRESENTS

Recycling programs
for this product may
not exist in your area.

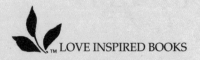 ™ LOVE INSPIRED BOOKS

ISBN-13: 978-0-373-48720-2

SWEET ON THE COWGIRL

www.Harlequin.com

Printed in U.S.A.

Honor your father and your mother,
so that you may live long in the land
the Lord your God is giving you.
—*Exodus* 20:12

Train a child in the way he should go,
and when he is old he will not turn from it.
—*Proverbs* 22:6

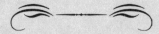

For our little daredevil, Brystol Olivia Zediker.
Grandma loves you!

Chapter 1

Dread bubbled inside of Guy Roberts. The filling-station attendant had said the Wild West show was setting up in the fairgrounds a half mile from Cottonwood Landing, Nebraska. This had to be the place. Although no signs advertised Cowboy Jack's Western Extravaganza, a dozen hands fenced off a rodeo arena while others raked dirt, hammered tent stakes into the ground and assembled bleachers.

He grimaced and eased his brand-new car, a 1924 Durant Star Speedster, into the grassy pasture. Peering through the windshield, he scanned the area for untethered horses. Satisfied he wouldn't meet one of the wild beasts face to face, he killed the engine, opened his car door and slid from behind the wheel.

The putrid scent of sun-warmed horse flesh mixed with their waste assaulted his nostrils, assuring him they were out of sight but in close proximity. His racing heart weakened his legs and sheened a cold sweat across his forehead. His stomach lurched, threatening to spill his breakfast on to the grassy ground. Guy placed his right arm on the ledge of the car roof and rested his clammy forehead against the rough tweed of his suit jacket. He swallowed hard, hoping to take control of his stomach and the fear squeezing his insides.

"Do you need help?"

Guy's body jerked. He'd seen no one in the immediate area when he pulled into the pasture.

"I'm sorry. I didn't mean to startle you. Are you ill?"

He'd been concentrating so hard on controlling his overpowering fright he hadn't heard the woman approach. The gentle lilt of her voice held more than an apology. Her sweet tones of motherly concern were a balm, easing his quivering fears and reminding him of his mother, the model example of a woman who put home and family first.

"I'm fi…" Looking up and turning, surprise widened his eyes and silenced him. The woman who stood before him was quite the opposite of the matronly image conjured up by his imagination. A petite girl, at least three years younger than his twenty-three years, stood behind him with a smile brighter than the gleaming chrome on his new car.

The flower accent on her straw cloche hat matched the pink background of her in-vogue pink-and-gray-print broadcloth dress. The wide, loose fold at the drop waistline created the illusion of a middy blouse over a form-fitting skirt.

How out of place she looked in the middle of the pasture decked out in the latest fashion! He'd assumed the women associated with the Western Extravaganza show dressed in buckskin-fringed riding skirts and vests. But this young lady looked like she should be window shopping on Fourth Street in downtown Sioux City, Iowa, not crossing a grassy range in nowhere Nebraska. This lovely young miss was a very pleasant surprise.

When she drew her brows together and narrowed her eyes, Guy's manners snapped into action. He tipped his homburg and bowed slightly. "I beg your pardon, miss. I didn't mean to stare. Could you tell me if this is where I can find Jack Barnes?" Hat still in hand he swept his arm wide.

A soft breeze rustled the strings of the bow accent on her dress and lifted the ends of her bobbed auburn hair that peeked out from under her hat. "It's Jonathan Barnes." Her rose-tinted lips curved into a smile. She held out a delicate hand. "I'm his daughter, Laura."

"Guy Roberts. Please excuse my bad manners. I'm a little out of sorts today." Not to mention out of place standing in the center of a pasture instead of sitting in a deep leather chair in his family's manufacturing office. His fear, which had dissipated with the appearance of Laura, reared up. Once again, his insides swirled.

He returned his hat to his head, sliding it back to expose his forehead to the cool breeze, hoping to dry his fear-induced cold sweat. Then he reached for Laura's hand.

The softness of her skin trailed across his hand, surprising him for the second time. Her fingers tightened around his as she shook with a firmer grip than most men he knew.

"Are you all right?" Laura furrowed her brow and crinkled her nose, moving the smattering of freckles across the bridge closer together. Guy's insides swirled again at Laura's touch.

She tugged her hand free of his sooner than he expected. His instincts urged him to recapture it, bring it to his lips and plant a kiss on her palm. In an effort to control his feelings he drew a deep steadying breath, forgetting the horse-scented air. The acidic scent burned his nostrils and permeated his tongue. He coughed, covering his mouth, and turned from Laura in an attempt to compose himself.

Lord, I am trying to obey Your commandment and honor my mother even though I don't understand her wish to have a trick rider sponsor our product. Please help ease my fears.

Pleasant warmth seeped through his jacket where Laura rested her palm against his back. Calm washed through him.

"Let's get you out of the hot sun. The office tent is this way." Laura placed a hand on his forearm and began to guide him across the grass to a grove of cottonwood trees. "You can sit down there and drink a glass of cool water."

Guy stopped walking and took shallow breaths through his mouth to filter the stench in the air. It didn't help his lightheadedness. "My briefcase is in the car."

"Oh. You wait here. I'll get it."

Before Guy could protest, Laura seemed to glide across the short spans of pasture. Her posture and poise rivaled that of the finest ballerina. Traipsing across uneven ground in her T-strap heels never threw off her balance. She seemed so out of place here, not at all what he expected in a showman's daughter. Perhaps she had attended an Eastern boarding school.

He marveled at the way Laura swung his attaché case, filled with twelve bottles of Papa Fizzy's Cream Soda, like an empty berry basket. Where would a petite gal get this much strength? More important, why would she want it?

Striding past him, she pointed with her free hand. "This way."

It took Guy a few quick steps to catch up with Laura. Flanking her left side where she carried his case, he swung his arm simultaneously with hers before reaching for the leather handle. "I'll carry that."

"If you're not feeling well, it's really no bother." Laura kept walking and swinging.

Guy managed to slip his right hand around the handle of the case, looping his fingers over Laura's. Her silky skin tickled his palm.

She turned her head toward him and smiled. "Are you sure?"

At his nod, she released her grasp on the handle at the same time his foot dropped into a rut. Guy quickly stumble-stepped. The swinging momentum of the case jolted him sideways and the handle slipped from his hand. Glass rattled as the case bounced on the ground.

"Oh, no." Laura knelt beside the attaché. "I hope whatever is in there didn't break."

Guy hesitated a moment; he didn't relish getting grass stains on the knees of his Oxford bags. But there wasn't any other option. He needed to open the case and check for breakage. He knelt beside Laura.

The case had landed upside down. Guy carefully turned it over. No sticky liquid oozed through the opening, which had to be a good sign.

"What's in there?"

Laura craned her neck over his shoulder, her breath like fluttering butterfly wings on his cheek.

"Papa Fizzy's Cream Soda." Guy flipped the end latches and slowly opened the case. He lifted a heavy towel to reveal twelve clear bottles filled with amber liquid, lying on their side on top of another thick towel.

"Are any broken?" Laura lightly touched a bottle.

"None appear to be." Guy picked one up, held it toward the sun and turned it.

"They were well padded." Laura lifted a bottle and inspected it. "This one's okay. Do you want to sell your soda pop at the show's concessions? Is that why you're here to see my dad?" Laura carefully returned her bottle to the case, then removed another one.

"No, well, yes. I mean—" Guy put the bottle back into the case and rubbed his hands across the rough tweed on his thighs.

He was an accountant. It's what he'd studied in college in preparation for working in the family business. "I'm here because we, I mean Papa Fizzy's, hopes your trick rider, Pete Barnes, wants to endorse our product. If he agrees, then yes, we'd want our cream soda sold in the concessions."

Guy turned to find Laura wide-eyed and flushed. He stuffed the padding back over the bottles and clicked the latches closed. "I believe we both need to get out of the hot August sun." Guy glanced around the pasture to ensure no horses were present.

He stood and extended his hand to assist Laura to her feet. She waved it off and with a quick jump, stood erect.

"Do you think your father would be interested in this type of business deal?"

Laura drew her mouth into a pucker and shrugged. "The tent's this way." She lifted a hand toward the grove of cottonwood trees.

They walked side by side at a pace much slower than before, the breeze bringing intermittent but faint wafts of horse stench. Guy relaxed, certain they were putting distance between them and the horses. "Is Pete a relative?"

Laura gave him a sideways glance. "He's my brother."

"I hear he's quite a talent."

"Yes." Laura's smile grew tight. "He's quite a talent, all right."

Guy stifled a smile at the obvious show of sibling rivalry. "I'm told he's the only trick rider brave enough to perform the back drag." Personally, Guy felt you'd have to be crazy, rather than brave, to perform tricks on a moving horse, but their company and his mother were depending on him to place this endorsement, so he'd have to keep his personal commentary to himself.

Laura's smile pulled tighter and she worried the decorative bow of her dress. "Bravery hasn't anything to do with it. Talent and practice allow any trick rider to perform the stunt correctly."

They rounded the grove and stepped into a clearing. Tents, horse trailers and various Model T trucks dotted the grass at the tree line. Women pinned clothes to ropes stretched between low-hanging tree limbs while children frolicked, darting under sheets and through the legs of stiff denim jeans drying on the line.

"The office is over there." Laura pointed to a large white tent set off a distance from the gypsy-type camp. Most of the women greeted Laura while giving Guy a scrutinizing once-over.

As Guy and Laura continued toward the tent, the honeysuckle fragrance she wore wafted toward him with her every movement—a delightful contrast to the Wild West show's aroma. Guy breathed deeply, filling his lungs with Laura's refreshing fragrance.

Keeping his eyes on the uneven ground, Guy cast sideways glances at Laura. She was at the age when a girl's cuteness turned into a woman's beauty. Pretty, graceful, dignified and refined, she had all of the makings of a fine lady.

Still, she seemed so out of place here. The women around the camp wore cotton house dresses; a few even sported trousers. She must be here on summer vacation from a school in the city. As he cast another glance toward her, Laura's gaze met his. Her deep brown eyes searched his face.

He needed to break the awkward silence surrounding them. "So what makes this trick so dangerous?"

Splaying her fingers in front of her and slowly moving her hands outward, a genuine smile brightened Laura's face. Her brown eyes twinkled. "Hanging on only by boots in the stirrups, the rider falls over the back of the horse until both hands dangle beside the horse's tail. Then the rider pulls back up into a sitting position."

A shiver of fear quaked Guy's insides. "I guess it is a dangerous trick!" His voice megaphoned through the pasture, creating an echo and drawing the attention of the workers. Why would anyone want to ride one of those beasts, let alone hang over the backside?

Laura waved her right hand dismissively through the air. "That's not the dangerous part. The danger of the trick is the rider isn't in control of the horse once letting go of the reins, and if the horse's hooves come up high while running, the rider gets kicked in the head."

Dizziness washed over Guy. He swayed. His grip on the case loosened. He stopped walking. Who in their right mind would do that for a living? He set the case on the ground, removed his handkerchief from his breast pocket and wiped his brow. Why had his mother insisted on sending him here? She knew he feared horses. He needed to secure Pete Barnes's signature and return to the city where he belonged.

When Laura realized he'd stopped walking, she turned and retraced her steps. Concern etched her face and she opened her mouth to speak.

Guy held up a silencing hand. "Has that ever happened?" Fear crackled his voice. His heart thundered in his chest like fierce hooves galloping against the hard ground.

"What?"

He swiped the soft cotton over his face, the rough stitching of the monogram scratched across his cheek. Did he really want to know?

"You mean the trick go bad?" Laura stepped closer, placing her hand on his shoulder.

Guy's eyes locked on Laura. He managed a nod.

"Not if the horse is well trained." Laura's kind smile returned. "Sorry, I might have added too much drama to my description, but I'm used to selling it to customers. It's our main attraction. The truth is—" Laura leaned her head closer to Guy in a conspiratorial stance and lowered her voice "—the horse is really the star of the trick, not the rider."

Laura's eyes sparkled. "Wait until you see my, I mean our, Starlight. She's the best and most beautiful horse you'll ever set eyes on. Should we go over to the fairground stable after your meeting with Dad? Once you see her, I think you'll want to include her in the endorsement advertisements."

He hadn't considered meeting the horse, only the rider. Guy gulped. "Well, maybe I should see how the meeting goes first. Mr. Barnes may not be interested." He wanted to spend more time with Laura but not looking at horses. Maybe a nice dinner and a walk through a park.

"I have a feeling he will be." Laura's smile turned sly. "We'll never know if we don't go ask him." Laura started toward the tent.

Guy returned his handkerchief to his pocket, lifted the case and caught up with Laura as she paused by the tent opening. "I need a moment." He set his case down, then brushed the dust from the knees of his trousers. He ran his hands across his double-breasted suit jacket to ensure it was buttoned properly. He raised his hat and ran his fingers through his hair before he returned it to the proper position on his head. "I'm ready." He picked up his case.

Laura lifted the flap and stepped through the opening.

Guy followed her through the canvas door, stopping for a second to let his eyes adjust to the shaded interior.

"Dad, a salesman is here to see you." Laura stepped aside to allow a better view of Guy.

The large man sitting behind the rough wooden table stood. A plaid cotton shirt pulled across his broad shoulders. Although tall, he was trim and wore his high-waist trousers well. His sandy hair, short and curly, hung in a style all its own. Mr. Barnes didn't fit the cowboy image Guy had fixed in his mind, either, although a straw cowboy hat did dangle precariously off the decorative end-tip on the straight-backed chair he'd risen from.

"Mr. Barnes, I'm Guy Roberts with Papa Fizzy's Cream Soda Company located in Sioux City, Iowa." Guy held his free hand out, meeting Mr. Barnes halfway around the table.

"Pleased to meet you. Call me Jack."

Guy's brow pulled in confusion.

"Dad, you should go by your Christian name, Jonathan." Laura's lips pulled into a reprimanding frown.

"Laura, when the good Lord calls my name, I'll answer to Jonathan. Until then, I'm going by Jack." His exasperation was evident. He gave his daughter a curt nod and turned his attention back to Guy.

Guy didn't miss seeing Laura cross her arms over her chest and give her dad a raised-eyebrow stare.

"What can I do for you, Mr. Roberts?"

"Please call me Guy. Papa Fizzy's is looking for someone to endorse our product." Guy hoisted his case higher and used it to motion toward the table where Jack had been sitting. "May I?"

Jack nodded his approval and followed Guy. Hefting the attaché to the table, Guy popped the locks and pulled out a bottle of cream soda.

"Our company hopes to partner with Pete Barnes to advertise our soda pop."

"You realize he means Buckskin Jones, the pony express rider." Laura stood to Guy's left and rapped her fingers on the table. She appeared to stare straight through him while she spoke to her father.

An exasperated sigh bounced off of the canvas tent's walls. "Of course I know he means the character." Jack gave Laura a pointed look and took the bottle of soda from Guy.

"Please try it, although I'm afraid it's warm now." Guy removed a second bottle and tipped it toward Laura. "You're welcome to try it, too." Guy produced a bottle opener from his pants pocket, hoping the drink sampling would deflect some of the tension between father and daughter.

"Ladies first." Guy popped the metal cork-lined bottle cap off the cream soda Laura held. She put it to her lips, taking a dainty sip.

"It's very good." She smiled at Guy, then pulled a longer drink from her bottle. Her eyes fluttered closed, long red lashes rested against her sun-kissed skin. How would it feel to trace his finger down her cheek?

When Guy felt the opener being pulled from his hand, he remembered Jack was waiting for a drink, too. "I'm so sorry, sir." Guy fumbled with the opener but managed to pop the cap off Jack's bottle of soda.

"Yum, Pete will do it." Laura licked her lips before brushing the back of her hand against them.

"Pete will do what?" A lanky cowboy stood inside the tent flap for a moment before he ambled over to the table and peered into the leather case.

He stood about three inches taller than Laura and there was no denying they were siblings. Their hair was the same shade of auburn, their features almost identical, except Pete's freckles spanned his entire face and not just the bridge of his nose. In the dim light he appeared to be younger. This could be a problem. If he wasn't at least sixteen, Jack would have to sign all the legal documents for him.

"Mr. Roberts wants Buckskin Jones to endorse Papa Fizzy's cream soda." She gave her brother a pointed look. "Guy Roberts, this is Pete Barnes, alias Buckskin Jones." Her intonation in the introduction suggested annoyance.

Shifting his weight from his left leg to his right, Pete removed his straw cowboy hat. So far he was the only member of this family who appeared to belong in a Western show, from his red bandana neckerchief down to the pointed toes of his scuffed brown boots. No wonder he was the main attraction.

Pete extended his hand. "Nice to meet you."

"Likewise." Guy fought a frown. Pete's weak hand-shake was almost over before it began, unlike the firm grasp of his father and sister. That would have to change. Papa Fizzy's expected Pete to reflect strength in his trick-riding skill and their product. He'd be expected to make public appearances, so his handshake needed to be firm and confident.

"I agree with Laura—it's mighty tasty." Jack passed his bottle to Pete.

Pete gulped a big swig and nodded. "Do I get free soda if I do it?"

The question caught Guy off-guard. He'd only brought along a boilerplate contract. Most of their endorsers signed the contracts, posed for ads, met with the public and, of course, cashed their paychecks. They didn't make any demands.

Chapter 2

"It doesn't matter, Pete. You're doing it."

Pete's head snapped up at Laura's commanding tone. "Yeah, yeah, sure I'll do it." Pete stammered while a sad veil covered his brown eyes.

"Now, hold on." Jack broke in. "Guy needs to go over the contract and details before any decisions are reached. Let's pull up a couple of chairs and visit about this offer."

Laura fumed over to the edge of the tent where three extra straight-backed chairs sat. She didn't need to hear the details. Buckskin Jones was signing the endorsement contract. The Wild West show could use an infusion of cash and so could the coffee can stashed away in her hope chest. In a few short months, she'd be twenty-one and then if her dad didn't let her perform under her own name, she'd find another traveling show that would.

Women were headlining trick-riding shows all across

America; some even toured Europe. If her dad would just listen to her, their show would be prospering and they'd be setting up in a big city, like Sioux City or Omaha, not a small county fairground in between. She tried to convince him, showing him magazine interviews and pictures of other female trick-riding stars, but he disapproved of their attire and insisted their reputations outside of the arena were tarnished.

So the talent God gave her, the perfect execution of the back drop, was credited to her brother Pete. She hated donning the binder she wore under the buckskin suit to flatten her chest into a boyish shape. It hurt to watch spectators surround Pete after a performance, patting his back and showering him with accolades for an awe-inspiring performance.

Bitter tears covered the surface of her eyes. It wasn't fair.

Laura sniffled and wiped the moisture from her eyes. No time for tears today. Signing the contract and collecting the pay was the first step to her freedom.

"Are you all right, sis?" Pete laid a hand on her shoulder.

Nodding in short, quick jerks, she glanced over her shoulder at her brother.

"Don't worry, sis. I'll sign the contract. I know the show needs the money. You grab one chair and I'll bring these two."

Stepping aside, she watched Pete grasp the back spindle of a chair with his left hand, then struggled to get a good hold on another one with his right hand. When he was eight years old a horse had bucked him. He landed wrong and broke his wrist. Even under a doctor's care, it didn't heal right and left him without much grip in his right hand. It was a blessing he was left-handed.

It was a double blessing no one had noticed Buckskin Jones holds the reigns with his right hand during the performance while Pete signed autographs with his left afterward.

"I've got it." Laura gently patted Pete's forearm. He'd tried so hard to regain use of his hand.

"Thanks, sis."

Laura smiled at Pete. None of this was his fault. She knew he hated pretending to be Buckskin Jones. Hopefully, in a few short months, the situation would change. Sooner if their father accepted the endorsement deal.

Pete offered the chair he carried to Guy, then took one of the chairs Laura carried and set it next to Guy before flopping down on the pressed cardboard seat.

Disappointment slipped through Laura. She'd wanted to sit by Guy. She needed to be able to read the contract, and, well, she found him dapper and handsome.

Of course, the chair placement helped keep the family secret. Guy might question why she was involved in the contract negotiations. Laura listened, making mental notes of the upfront money and percentage of profits. This was what their Wild West show needed, providing Buckskin Jones lured people to drink Papa Fizzy's Cream Soda. A pretty girl dressed in red leather riding breeches with a matching vest adorned with white stars and spangles complemented by a white satin blouse would be more eye-catching in ads…if Papa Fizzy's created colored ads.

"Young man—" Jack's bass rumbled around the tent, drawing Laura from her internal plans "—we'll need to read over the contract and discuss it in private. It seems equitable, but I'm not a man who rushes into anything."

"All right. That's fair." Guy's slight hesitation before he glanced over his shoulder at the tent opening was an odd reaction to her father's statement. Turning back to the group, his smile tightened, giving it the appearance of a grimace. He gave a slight nod.

Laura scooted to the edge of her chair, itching to grab the contract and read it. "I was explaining to Guy how I think Starlight should appear with Buckskin Jones in the print ads and during personal appearances. Children and adults always enjoy petting Starlight after a performance." *In addition to pouring out accolades on Pete.*

Guy's body jerked. His eyes opened wide. "Wouldn't having a horse around spectators be dangerous?"

Laura detected a slight quiver in his voice.

He cleared his throat and looked from Laura to her father. "Our contract doesn't allow for the horse."

"Starlight."

"I beg your pardon?" He turned back to Laura.

"Not *the* horse, Starlight. She has a name. I told you earlier, she is a star in her own right. And I don't understand what you mean by dangerous."

"A horse around women and children… If someone got hurt…disaster for the show…liability for our company." Guy hung his head.

Laura had trouble catching every word of his whispered stammer. Was he implying Starlight would hurt women and children? She pursed her lips tight to keep from smiling and almost snorted in a most unladylike way. Starlight was gentle and well mannered, another reason to not give up on her point. "Well, get Starlight added to the contract or it's no deal."

"Sis." Pete turned to her. Confusion etched his features.

Guy's head snapped up at the firmness of Laura's voice. His brow creased. He drew a deep breath and released it with a harrumph. "Miss Barnes, I don't really see how any of this is your concern." Guy turned back to her father and Pete.

Angry flames ignited in Laura's chest. Of course he didn't see how any of this was her concern. If her father would bill her as the trick rider, this wouldn't be a problem. She had every right to make the decisions for Buckskin Jones, although no one outside their family knew that.

Poor Pete. She'd just told him to sign the contract no matter what and now she insisted on the opposite. She tapped Pete's shin with the toe of her shoe.

He jumped and sat up straight, innocent eyes meeting her glare. With pursed lips she jerked her head toward Guy.

Pete stammered, "Na…na…na…no deal if Starlight isn't included."

"Now, Pete." Her dad looked up from the contract he'd been reading. His pointed gaze passed Pete by and settled on her. "Let's not be too demanding. Mr. Roberts's offer is very fair. It's a sizable sum of money."

"Does this mean the contract meets your approval?"

Laura could tell by the delight in Guy's voice that he felt the negotiations were over. She said, "There is no Buckskin Jones act without Starlight." *Or me.* "So it is only fair she appear in some of the endorsements. Besides, I thought we were going to review the contract in private."

Guy turned to Laura, a sweet smile on his face. "Miss Barnes, it's apparent Starlight is your horse."

Laura narrowed her eyes. Had Guy shivered when he said the word horse?

"But Papa Fizzy's has no intention of placing a horse in our endorsements. However, the contract we are offering your brother is more than generous. I can assure all of you the only Western act receiving higher endorsement pay is…"

The pallor drained from Guy's face and he swallowed hard. Clearing his throat he finished his sentence. "Winona Phelps."

Winona Phelps! She was an amateur compared to Laura. Winona's horse barely broke a trot as she clumsily went through her routine.

"How do we know for sure?" Pete's question broke through Laura's thoughts.

"Excuse me?" Guy turned his attention to Pete.

"How do we know what you said is true?"

"That's a very good question, Pete. I'm agreeable if you and your father want to verify my statements before signing the contract. I have nothing to hide. I stated a commonly known fact. Winona Phelps makes almost twice that amount."

Laura's father let out a whistle. "Why?"

Guy shrugged. "A woman trick rider provides more thrills to the crowd."

Exactly what I've been trying to tell you. Laura stood, seeing her opening. She cleared her throat, crossed her arms over her chest and arched a brow at her dad. "I think we should verify what Mr. Roberts said."

There was no way Buckskin Jones was signing the contract now. This could be the leverage she needed to convince her dad to drop the Buckskin Jones character and make Laura Barnes, the All-American Girl, the headlining act.

Her dad met her arched-brow stare with one of his own, then rolled his eyes to the side.

Following her dad's cue, Laura saw that Pete sat with his eyes downcast. Guy's astonishment was apparent as he took turns looking from one Barnes to another.

Laura saw that Guy seemed to be trying to figure out why Pete, the headliner, showed disinterest. Poor Pete hated being dragged through the disagreements between her and her dad. Also, if she didn't back off now, their secret might be revealed.

"Pete." Laura put the silk back into her voice. "Isn't that what you want to do? Verify what Mr. Roberts said before you sign the contract?"

When her brother's eyes met hers, she smiled. Pete's gentleness matched Starlight's. He didn't deserve being put in the middle of this. If only her dad could see that.

"I would. If that's all right with you, Mr. Roberts? This is such an honor to be asked to be sponsored by your soda-pop company, but I need some time to absorb everything it entails and check a few things out." Pete rubbed his palms up and down his jeans.

"The mark of a good businessman." Guy stuck his hand out and smiled. "I am confident you'll find we are in line with other acts of your caliber. Why don't I give you a couple of weeks to check things out? When I return, I'm sure you'll want to sign the contract." Guy rapped his knuckles on the wooden table, and for the first time since Laura laid eyes on his handsome face, he appeared relaxed.

"Actually, Mr. Roberts, I think you should stick around the Wild West show. Do a little firsthand research yourself. We might not be the right fit for your company."

"I can assure you that's not necessary. Our scouts were thorough before they made the suggestion to our sales department." Guy waved off her father's comment.

"That's a wonderful idea!" Laura clapped her hands together. "You can meet Starlight. Once you see her I'm certain you'll change your mind about not allowing her in the endorsement photos. Starlight's a beautiful paint."

The tension returned to Guy's features, pushing all the color from his face. "Thank you, but no. I'm sure the company needs me back in the city."

Disappointment fluttered through Laura. She wanted to spend more time with Guy to question him about business matters. Her father had told her horror stories of entertainers being swindled out of their earnings by underhanded managers. She wanted to find out of if they were true or just a scare tactic.

"Although—" Guy stood and began to remove the bottles from his attaché, setting them on the table "—I do need a room for tonight. Can you recommend an accommodation?" He looked at her father.

"I'm sure the Huntington where we're staying has vacancies." Laura clasped her hands. She'd get to spend some time with Guy after all and hopefully get answers to her questions.

"The Huntington sounds wonderful." Guy's bright smile made his eyes sparkle. Laura's heart pattered while she basked in the appreciation glowing in Guy's cobalt blue eyes.

"Ahem." Only *her* father could inflect sternness in a simple throat clearing.

Guy broke their gaze.

"There are other nice establishments in town, Mr. Roberts."

"But—" Laura tucked her hands behind her back and strolled behind Guy "—none are quite as nice as the Huntington." The only consolation her father had given her in this little trick-riding ruse was she didn't have to board in a tent or trailer. The family stayed in a suite in the hotel nearest to the show. "They have a wonderful dining room and serve breakfast, lunch and dinner. Each room has a private bath."

Her father evidently sensed her interest in Guy. His eyes bore down on her, conveying his constant warning: Think of your reputation. Yet he'd be surprised at why she was interested in Guy.

"Sounds swell." The metal clasps on Guy's case clicked closed. "Do you mind giving me directions?"

"Directions? I'll take you there myself. That's where I was heading when I ran into you earlier."

Guy looked from her father to her. "Laura, I'd be happy to have you escort me to town and join me for dinner, but only if it's all right with your father."

If it were up to her father, she'd never be alone with a man. He seldom granted her permission to accept a date. Her shoulders sagged a little. She needed to talk business with Guy *alone* and for longer than the short ride in to town. Dinner would be perfect. She flipped her hand in the air. "This isn't a date, just business, Dad."

Her father shot her a skeptical look and put both hands on his hips. "I guess so. Don't let her wrangle you into the fanciest hotel. The town offers several nice places to stay that are more reasonably priced."

"Thank you, sir." Guy reached out his hand. "It was very nice to meet you. The office number is in the contract in the event you need to speak to me before I return in a couple of weeks."

Laura stepped aside while Guy shook her father's and then Pete's hand.

"See you later." Laura wiggled her fingers at her family and led the way out of the tent.

"Although I'm delighted by your company, I'm certain I could find the hotel on my own. I don't want to keep you from something pressing."

"Oh, you're not." Laura and Starlight practiced every morning before sunup to ensure no one would see, leaving the remainder of her day free.

Laura deliberately headed toward the pasture where Guy had parked his car. She wanted to prolong their time together, get some answers to her questions. And this was her first opportunity. Laura turned and realized Guy wasn't walking alongside her.

Stopping, she twisted around. Guy stood right outside of the tent flap, intently looking around the area. Uncertainty etched his features. Was he reconsidering the offer? Thinking their operation wasn't up to par?

"We just started to set up the show for the fall season." Her tone was a little more terse than she'd intended. Their Western show was truly an extravaganza even with decades-old equipment. Her father and Pete built colorful props. She sewed dazzling costumes—except for her own.

Mopping his brow, Guy walked over to her. "I know your father runs an amazing show. Papa Fizzy's did extensive research on several traveling shows."

Silently they fell into a comfortable pace and began to retrace their steps through the pasture.

"Were all of them Wild West shows?" Laura knew their competition, and their Western show offered more entertainment than most.

"No." Guy huffed. He craned his neck before continuing. "We looked at a circus performer and a race-car driver, but my mother loves Western movies so the Wild West shows really appealed to her." Guy gave his head a small shake. "I don't quite understand her fascination."

Laura smiled. She did. Western lore romanced the adventurous nature buried deep in people's hearts. That's why their show was a success. For two hours they reenacted stagecoach robberies and buckboard races, giving regular folks a taste of what the pioneers had experienced.

"The conquering of the West appeals to many people."

"My mother is a testament to that fact."

They walked into the clearing where Guy's car sat at the edge of the pasture.

"Do you want to meet Starlight now?"

"No!"

Laura's head snapped sideways. She drew her brows together at the disgust in Guy's voice.

Guy cleared his throat. "No, thank you." He smiled, although it looked forced. "I'd better get into town and secure a room for the evening. I need to call the office to let them know how the negotiations are proceeding and tell them I gave your father two weeks to decide."

They reached the car. Guy opened the passenger door and stowed his attaché behind the front seat, then motioned for Laura to sit.

"So what made you decide to offer Buckskin Jones a sponsorship?" Laura smoothed her skirt and slipped on to the seat.

"It was between your show and Colonel Cooper's…"

Laura snorted. "Winona Phelps."

"Yes, Winona Phelps."

"Were we your second choice because another company swooped in and offered her a contract?"

"Well…"

Guy breathed hesitation into one word. Laura raised her brows in expectancy.

"Yes and no. Your outfit was my mother's second choice. Buckskin Jones was my first choice."

Laura smiled at his admission. Her trick riding was impressive even in a manly costume.

"Mother likes the idea of a woman trick rider."

A tickle of hope looped through her. Perhaps this was the answer to her prayers. If a sponsor preferred a woman trick rider, maybe it would convince her father to change his mind. She smiled wider. "I'm glad you chose our show. What influenced your decision?"

"If our company is going to sponsor a trick rider, it needs to be a man. I don't think it's a good idea for a woman to be doing dangerous tricks on the back of a moving horse."

Laura's heart plummeted.

Chapter 3

Guy paced across the plush area rug in the center of the hotel lobby. He pulled his pocket watch from his vest and popped the cover. Less than five minutes had passed since the last time he'd checked.

His life seemed to revolve around waiting on women. He'd phoned Mr. Turner, the company's chief accountant, hours ago in hopes of speaking with him, but he had been unavailable. Then he called his mother and left a detailed message with Ethel, her social secretary.

Guy sighed. He hoped the message his mother received was in fact the one he conveyed. Ethel seldom relayed the message as it was intended.

He looked down at his still opened watch. Ten minutes after the hour. A thread of anxiety rippled through him. Had Laura changed her mind about dinner? She'd grown sullen on the short ride into town. When he'd asked her to meet him in the lobby at six o'clock to join him for dinner, she bit her lower lip and nodded her head before quickly ascending the stairs to her family's suite.

Perhaps her father had changed his mind, contacted her and forbade her to join him. There was tension between father and daughter. The subtle answers and pointed looks were all too familiar for Guy to miss.

Only in his case it was mother and son.

Movement at the top of the stairs caught Guy's eye. He stopped pacing and looked at the wide staircase, hoping to see Laura. Instead, an elderly man and woman gingerly descended.

Guy started to turn away when Laura appeared at the top of the staircase. His sharp intake of breath resounded through the high ceiling of the lobby, probably causing stares. Yet he kept his eyes fixed on the beautiful girl peering over the thick, oak stair rail.

When Laura's gaze met his, a wide smile brightened her face. After waiting for the elderly couple to finish their decent, Laura seemed to glide down the stairs.

Mesmerized by her beauty, her tardiness no longer mattered to Guy. Her straight hair, cut in a stylish bob, swayed with every step.

She'd changed into a white sailor-style middy blouse. The band of the long top skimmed her hips and held the wide, neat pleats of her navy skirt, which brushed her shapely gams right below her knee, in place. The sailor collar started at a V-neckline and draped across her shoulders; the squared edge hit her mid-back. The loose ends of a mock tie sported a perfect nautical knot in the front.

The large collar flapped with each tap of her toes on the stairs. Her grace and balance were incredible. Laura's hand never touched the thick carved stair banister, nor did she tip her head down to watch her feet.

Her perfect posture captivated him. She must have graduated at the top of her class in finishing school.

In seconds she stood in front of him. The top of her head barely reached his shoulder. She tilted back her head.

"Are you still feeling out of sorts?" Her eyes roved his face. "If so, we can cancel our supper plans."

Guy studied her pretty features. She was sincere in her offer to break their dinner date if he wasn't feeling well. What a refreshing quality.

"I'm feeling much better and think a nice nourishing dinner is just what I need." Not only was Laura a pretty girl, but also a caring one. Most of the city girls in his social circles were polished to perfection on the outside but lacked sincerity in their words and actions.

She pursed her lips and narrowed her eyes, obviously determining if he was telling the truth. Then she smiled and rubbed her palms together. "Great. I'm starving."

Her hearty laugh shocked him more than her previous statement.

"You should see your face." Her laughter continued.

Heat burned his neck and licked his cheeks. He hadn't realized his expression showed his surprise. "The girls I know never admit they're hungry."

"I could tell by your flabbergasted features." Laura's laughter turned to a chuckle. "It's hard work practicing…"

Laura stopped. Placing her fingers over her lips, she drew brows together, furrowing her forehead.

"Practicing what?" Guy offered Laura his elbow.

Laura forced a smile and swallowed the truth before she blurted out their secret. She was Buckskin Jones. It took her all afternoon to work her anger at Guy's earlier statement down to a slight irritation. His opinions matched her father's. She disagreed with him, but like it or not, she had to spend time with him. She needed to pick Guy's brain for business information.

"I meant exercising."

"I see. Shall we?" Guy tipped his head toward the dining room door.

Pomade held his straight black hair, parted down the side, in place. He'd changed into a navy suit with a double-breasted jacket. The red stripes in his necktie were a perfect match to the piping around her sailor collar.

Guy's brows pulled together. He wiggled his elbow.

The last thing she wanted to do was take his arm, but she was a showman and used to playing a part. She drew a deep breath and smiled, resting her hand on his forearm in the way she'd seen a starlet hold her escort's arm in a movie magazine.

A smile lit Guy's handsome face. He really did cut a dashing figure in his dark suit.

"We make quite a patriotic pair in our red, white and blue attire. I'm not surprised, though. What could be more American than soda pop or a Wild West show?" she said.

Guy's brows twitched before he frowned.

What little confidence Laura had to pull off this escapade fell to the pit of her stomach. She spent all afternoon practicing phrases to turn polite conversation back to business. Not one of those scenarios covered aggravation, which is what twisted Guy's features.

Laura lowered her gaze and ground the toe of her T-strap into a pale pink rose on the lobby's large area rug. What had she said wrong? She replayed her sentence over in her mind. She'd said nothing wrong. As a matter of fact it would make a great advertising slogan.

She squared her shoulders and looked Guy in the eyes, beautiful cobalt-blue eyes, and forced herself to smile broadly. "Wouldn't that make a nice advertising campaign? Billing the Wild West show and Papa Fizzy's as being all American?" She waved her free hand through the air.

The tense expression remained fixed on Guy's face for a few more seconds, then he shrugged his shoulders. "That's not my area of expertise. I can run it past the advertising department. Once I'm done securing the contract, my job is finished. The advertising department will begin working on slogan and ad ideas."

He placed his hand over hers and slid it into the crook of his arm. "Let's not spoil our dinner talking about business." He led her toward the hotel dining room. "I hope you don't mind if we dine here. I'm expecting a phone call from my mother."

Guy pulled a gold pocket watch from his jacket, checked the time and shook his head. "I'd hoped to leave early in the morning and drive back to Sioux City, but until I'm able to speak with my mother…" Guy looked up and smiled. "Sorry, I said we wouldn't talk about business."

Panic reared up in her chest, weakening her limbs. She wanted to talk about business. She needed to encourage Guy to continue, certain he could provide information she'd need to know in a few months if she had to go out on her own. "It's quite all right. I don't mind talking about business. Besides, I did tell my father this was a business dinner."

Sheepishness crept into Guy's features, but his eyes

twinkled with happiness. "It'd please me if it was a date."

On a date with a handsome, sophisticated man instead of a rodeo cowboy? A thrill more intense than when the crowd cheered for her perfectly executed back drop wound its way through her.

Every ounce of her wanted to say "okay." She managed to shake her head. "Sorry, it has to be business." She didn't always agree with her father's rules or his insistence she pretend to be a man and let her brother take top billing at the Wild West show, but she did try to follow God's commandment and honor him. He'd provided a comfortable home and healed her heartbreak when her mother died.

"Well, what do we have here? Laura Barnes on a date? Does your father know?" The voice came from behind them. Laura didn't need to turn around. She recognized the twang in the drawl.

"What are you doing here, Clifford Hutton?" Laura didn't hide her suspicion.

Clifford walked around until he stood in front of her and Guy. He looked Guy up and down, then turned his gaze on Laura. His brown eyes stared deeply into hers. "You know very well why I'm here. I'm checking out my competition."

Wariness washed through Laura. She chuckled politely at Clifford's joke. "Pete's not here."

"Is he my competition?" Clifford feigned an innocent expression, then punctuated it with a wink.

Laura hoped Clifford's comment meant he thought his Roman riding act far outshone Buckskin Jones's talents. It had to be; he couldn't know their Buckskin Jones ruse. They'd been very thorough with their cover-up.

Guy cleared his throat.

"I'm sorry. Guy Roberts, this is Clifford Hutton." Laura pulled her hand free of Guy's arm. "Guy's company, Papa Fizzy's Cream Soda, wants Buckskin Jones to sign an endorsement contract." Everyone knew Clifford hankered for an endorsement deal. She flashed him a sly smile and watched the smugness drain from his expression.

"It's nice to meet you." Guy offered his hand to Clifford. "And what is it you do for a living?"

A giggle hiccupped from Laura before she could stop it. Clifford thought a lot of himself. He favored movie cowboy attire, wearing bright-colored Western shirts complete with fringe and pearl snaps. Today was no exception. His tall, black Stetson matched his pointed-toed black boots with a turquoise inlaid design. Black piping accented his shiny turquoise Western shirt. He did cut a nice-looking figure during a performance with his blond curly hair and expensive outfits.

"I'm a Roman rider. Perhaps you've heard of me?"

Clifford resembled a peacock the way he stuck his chest out waiting to be recognized and adored.

"I'm afraid not. Tell me, what does a Roman rider do?"

Quickly turning her head away from the men, Laura covered her mouth and coughed to stifle her laughter.

"A Roman rider is a rodeo performer who stands on the back of two paired horses—mine are white—and performs riding and roping tricks." Clifford didn't disguise his annoyance at having to explain his occupation.

"Oh."

Guy's one-word response sounded like a distain-filled grunt.

Laura turned back to the two men, who stared at each other with the same look of disbelief.

"What do you mean by that?" Clifford narrowed his eyes. He pushed his hat back a few inches, allowing a blond curl to fall across his forehead, and put his meaty hand on his hip.

Clifford showing up was going to wreck her plan to talk business with Guy. This might be her only chance to be alone with him.

"I'm not impressed with a man who makes his living…"

Laura stepped between the men, entwining her arm in Guy's. "I hate to interrupt, but I am famished." She smiled at Guy before turning to Clifford. "Always nice to see you, Cliff." She wiggled her fingers in a dismissive wave, knowing the use of the short form of his name only raised his dander higher.

Guy tipped his head, then led Laura toward the hotel's dining room.

Once they were seated and studying the menu, Guy looked up. "Order anything you wish. I know you're famished."

"Thank you."

"I surmise you've eaten here before?"

"Yes, several times." Laura peeked over the top of her menu. His blue eyes brighter than a Nebraska summer sky sent her heart skipping through her chest. The fluttering emotions inside of Laura whisked away her appetite.

"Any recommendations?" Guy arched his dark brows in question.

"The fried chicken is good. I mean, I enjoy it and so does Pete. But the meatloaf dinner is our favorite. Oh, and the pot roast melts in your mouth." Realizing she was ready to describe another blue plate special, Laura pursed her lips before she prattled on and uttered more nonsense. What was wrong with her? She never had trouble talking to the opposite sex.

"I believe I'll have the fried chicken on your recommendation." Guy laid his menu to the side and took a sip of water. "What may I order for you?"

Laura's eyes widened, glad her vision was riveted to her menu so Guy didn't see. Why would a woman want a man to order for her? She scrunched her face in confusion.

Six months short of twenty-one, she should know if this was standard date etiquette. Why had her father kept such a tight hold on her? Her frustration huffed out and vibrated the stiff paper menu.

"Having trouble deciding?"

Her head jerked up. Had her sigh been that loud?

Guy's bright smile greeted her, causing her heart to whirl faster than Pete's showman lariat.

"You might say that." Laura lifted her menu higher and scrunched her head down in her shoulders. She needed to buy some time to get her thoughts and emotions straightened out. She reminded herself of Guy's earlier comment about women trick riders. A thread of anger stitched her shoulders, straightening her posture. She couldn't forget what she was here for: information. She mustn't forget why Guy was in town: to offer them a lucrative endorsement. She closed her eyes.

Lord, I need Your gentle guidance. Please steady my emotions. Amen.

Laura drew a deep breath before opening her eyes. She lowered the closed menu and placed it on top of Guy's. "I believe I'll have the fried chicken, too."

Guy motioned the waiter over with a flick of his hand. She took several sips of her water to keep from interjecting and placing her own meal order. It seemed silly to her, but perhaps that's what the society ladies Guy spoke of preferred.

A twinge of longing started in the depth of her heart and rippled through her. Sewing and wearing fashionable clothes made her feel ladylike and helped her bear the agony of donning those manly buckskins, but she knew looking the part on the outside didn't really make her a lady.

She could learn, though. Maybe go to finishing school with her earnings. But first she needed business information from Guy.

"I noticed they don't offer your cream soda on the menu. Are you planning to make sales stops to other businesses while you're here?" Laura rested her arms, one over the other, on the table.

"No. I won't be in town long enough. My plan is to leave early in the morning to travel back to the city, but if I don't receive the call from my mother soon—" Guy fished out his pocket watch and checked the time again "—I may be changing my plans."

Laura knitted her brows. "I thought a salesman would stop at all of the shops and restaurants urging them to sell his product."

Tucking the watch back in his pocket, Guy leaned back in his chair. "Papa Fizzy's is a family-owned business like your Wild West show. I'm a schooled accountant, but Elmer Turner, our chief accountant, feels I should learn the business from the bottom up, the way my grandfather built it. My mother agrees, so here I am."

Guy lifted his hands palm out, showing his helplessness, a feeling Laura shared. He wanted control of his future, too.

Her heart softened a bit. She nodded.

"My mother doesn't seem to understand I'm better suited to an office position. I've learned all the new business techniques. I've even studied the stock market and how selling shares in our company could increase the capital and profits and move us from a regional company to a national company."

"So you've talked to her about this?" Laura leaned over her arms. He might share a tidbit, something that might help her convince her father to give her credit for the Buckskin Jones act.

"Yes. She says Mr. Turner is doing a fine job and the company doesn't need two accountants." Guy gave a small snort. "I don't know how, though, because he never seems to be in his office. I've tried to visit with him several times and he's either in meetings or away. He is an elusive employee."

The front desk clerk walked up to the table. "Excuse me, Mr. Roberts."

Guy began to rise. "Is there a phone call for me?"

"I'm afraid not. You received a telegram." He handed a sealed envelope to Guy, turned and walked away.

"Is it from your mother?"

"Yes." Standing now, Guy ripped open the envelope and pulled out the message. Deep lines creased his forehead and his lips tightened. He flopped back on the chair.

"Is everything all right?"

"No." Guy looked up at her. "Mother wants me to stay here until your brother signs the contract."

Chapter 4

Silence settled around their table. Guy's lips had pursed when he first read the telegram; now they pulled into a frown. How long was he going to stare at the telegram? Re-reading it wouldn't change the message.

Guy's unhappiness at his mother's request was apparent, but the message had the opposite effect on Laura. Guy's previous departure plans had put time constraints on her mission. His extended stay gave her more time to learn about the other endorsements offered to women trick riders. Plus, she could introduce him to Starlight. Once he saw what a gentle horse she was, he'd see the advantage of adding the mare to the advertisements.

Finally folding the paper, Guy tucked it into his jacket's inner pocket. His gaze met hers. The emotion reflecting from his eyes deepened the concern settling into the planes of his face. She swallowed hard. More than once her mirror had reflected the same expression after a confrontation with her father. Disappointment mixed with longing lassoed Laura's heart and cinched hard. Her earlier anger at Guy dissipated.

She started to reach across the table to clasp his hand to show him she, too, understood the difficulty in obeying God's commandment to honor your father and mother.

"Is everything all right here?"

Laura looked up into her father's brown eyes and caught the slight shake of his head. She pulled her hand back and dropped it in her lap, remembering what he'd taught her about public displays of affection being harmful to her reputation.

Affection? That wasn't why she wanted to comfort Guy. It was understanding. Laura squared her shoulders. "Guy received a telegram from his mother."

Her father turned his attention to Guy and knitted his brows. "I hope it wasn't bad news."

"She wants me to stay here until Pete signs the contract." Guy no longer frowned, but his raised brows creased his forehead in confusion.

"If it's a problem getting a room here for two weeks, there are other establishments…"

"I never thought about that." Guy's eyes brightened. "Perhaps an extended stay will be thwarted by the lack of a vacancy."

Laura and her dad exchanged a look.

"Oh, excuse me. I assure you I meant nothing by my comment. It's just I gave you two weeks to read and consider the contract. You can't possibly want me under foot for two weeks. And what would I do with my time?" Guy's kind smile returned.

"Do you have other sales calls to make in the area?" Laura's dad took off his cowboy hat and lightly tapped

Laura's shoulder before he took a seat across from her. She slid her chair a few inches away from Guy's.

"Actually, Guy is an accountant, not a salesman. He's here at his mother's request." Laura gave Guy a polite grin.

"That's why I'm so perplexed by her message. How will I fill my days?" Guy smiled at Laura, the sparkle returning to his cobalt eyes.

Laura's heart started its own trick-riding routine, flipping and bouncing at the appreciation dancing in Guy's eyes. Did he want to spend time with her during the day? Her face warmed. She tried to pull the reins on the corners of her lips, but like an uncontrolled horse, they broke into a wide smile.

"Ahem."

Laura broke their eye contact, casting a sideways glance at her father.

"An accountant?"

"Yes, we've been discussing how he's learning the family business from the ground up."

Some of the lines softened around her dad's eyes at her explanation. He'd done a fine job of raising her. She wished he'd give her a chance to prove it. He never seemed to trust her judgment, not with men or her career.

He gave her a slight nod and turned to Guy. "I'm a little behind on my bookkeeping for the show. It happens this time of year when we are setting up and tearing down every few weeks."

Laura watched her dad's stance change from formidable to false bravado. He leaned back on his chair in nonchalance. Her father's lack of education was another secret the Barnes family kept. Although he'd completed eighth grade, his reading and arithmetic skills were basic. The real reason he didn't jump into anything, including the contract Guy had offered them, is because he needed more time than most people to read and understand documents.

"I don't suppose you'd be interested in helping me out with them while you're here?"

To the untrained ear her father's question seemed casual. Laura heard the underlying hope in his words. He and Pete had been scouring the books for weeks thinking there was a mistake. They both thought the show should have more in the bank than their ledgers and the bank showed. Arithmetic wasn't Laura's long suit, either. She tried to help by honing her act to draw in bigger crowds, which would be easier to do if she could be billed as herself.

The swish of Guy rubbing his palms together drew Laura back into the conversation.

"I don't mind at all. Working with numbers is my passion."

"Great." Laura's father waved the waitress over to the table.

"Are you joining us for dinner?"

Laura gave Guy a weak smile and small shoulder shrug when his eyes darted from her father back to her. He was obviously disappointed with the addition of their supper mate, too, although not for the same reasons. Laura's business questions would have to wait for another day. Now that Guy was staying on for two weeks she knew she'd get her chance.

"It is a business dinner, isn't it?"

Her father delivered the simple question with a tone that implied he knew Guy felt this dinner was anything but business. How could he know that? Had he eavesdropped on their previous conversation? Laura crossed her arms over her chest and glared at her father, but her actions were in vain. He kept his gaze focused on Guy.

A blush deepened Guy's face. "You are quite right— it is a business dinner. We've already ordered. Perhaps the cook can keep our dinners warm so we can all enjoy our meal together. Is that acceptable to you, Laura? You did say you were famished."

Laura nodded. "Guy was just telling me how he longs to have a more active role in their family business."

"Really?" Her father cocked an eyebrow, her warning not to take this conversation any further.

"Involving the next generation in decision-making is the only way to ensure the family business continues on. Isn't it, Guy?" Laura knew her line of questioning might put Guy on the spot.

"Yes, that is correct." Guy took a sip of his water.

"There's one difference, Laura." Her father gave her a pointed look. "Guy is a man. It's not a woman's place to be involved in business decisions."

Fury looped through Laura. She was the headliner and should have some say in the business decisions, especially concerning the character she portrayed. She opened her mouth.

"I couldn't agree more. My mother's role in the family business is on the social side with parties and charity work. She softens the rough edges of the business, which gives us a nice standing in social circles. I'm sure, with your permission, of course, this is a role Laura could easily fill for your show to help attract business."

Laura could feel her eyes bug from the galloping anger inside of her. She pursed her lips to keep from blurting out that she *was* the one who attracted business.

"I'm sure she could. I'll consider it." Her father's

brown eyes twinkled with merriment when he winked at Laura.

His amusement at the situation brought a thin sheen of moisture to her eyes. At one time she thought their ruse was funny, too, but not anymore.

"Laura, are you all right?"

She met Guy's gaze and quickly nodded. His blue eyes swam with concern. If he didn't have such a strong opinion of women in business, it would have touched her heart. Instead, it swelled the hurt pressing down on her chest. She grabbed a glass of water and took a long drink to wash down the sob forming in her throat.

"Good morning." Guy arose from his station at the long table cluttered with ledgers, receipts and statements. "By the look on your face, your father didn't tell you we turned the common room of your suite into a makeshift office while I work on the show's book-keeping."

He glanced at Pete, who sat on the davenport leafing through a magazine. Pete looked at his sister, and his eyes widened slightly before his mouth turned down into a frown that matched Laura's. "I think I'll go to my room."

Pete's eyes met Guy's as he walked across the room to the bedroom door. The slight shake of his head gave Guy the indication that Laura had had no idea about the makeshift office. Two days before over breakfast, the men had made the decision. When Guy expressed his concern about disturbing Laura, Jack explained she always awoke early to call on some of the worker's wives or exercise the horses.

Guy shivered at the thought and watched Laura's gaze rove around the room, assessing the men's rearrangement of the furniture. He, Jack and Pete had moved the square, drop-leaf table to a spot in front of the window. The sun rays streaming through the long rectangular window would allow Guy to work in natural light most of the day.

They'd placed the small davenport and overstuffed chairs on the faded, oval rag rug covering the center of the linoleum flooring. The floor lamp cord could easily reach the table or the furniture to provide light for evening reading.

Based on his experience with his mother and because women had an eye for decorating, Guy had tried to persuade Jack to wait for Laura before they relocated the furniture. Jack assured him Laura wouldn't care about the room rearrangement.

"No, no he didn't." Laura finished walking across the threshold of the main door of the suite, closing it with a tad too much force. "I'm not surprised though. A woman has no place in business."

The defiant way Laura jutted her chin out after her statement lifted his heart. He liked a woman with spirit. "Ah, the reason for your silence during dinner the other evening surfaces. You don't share our opinion."

"No, I don't. You of all people, living in the city, should be aware of the suffrage movement." Laura pulled on the fingers of her lacy gloves, first removing one then repeating the same steps to remove the other. Her cloche hat was decorated with a green plaid ribbon, a perfect match to the color of her silk dress.

"I am well aware of the suffrage movement." Guy lifted his hand and rubbed his fingers over his mouth to hide his grin. Laura's dander gave her cheeks a very fetching color. "Some of the women in my mother's social circle are involved in those activities. It's a waste of their precious time. The bill allowing women to vote will never be ratified."

"Another subject we disagree on. Why aren't you out at the fairgrounds doing the bookkeeping work in the office tent?" Laura slipped off her hat. Tucking her gloves inside, she set it on the table beside a lamp. She ran her fingers through her hair. The soft red strands floated down to her jawline to frame her face in a fiery halo.

Fear's cold chill erased Guy's smile. He mustered his bravado to keep his voice from shaking. "I work better indoors." Relieved that his voice sounded natural, he exhaled.

Laura's crinkled nose spurred him on. "It's quieter here. I can concentrate on the figures." He'd had this same conversation with Jack Barnes a few days ago. It might be an excuse, but it wasn't a lie. He'd never get work done in a tent near horses, and working with numbers did require a person's full attention.

"Wouldn't it help to have Dad close by in case you have a question?" Laura walked over to the table and ran her fingers across the edge.

Of course it would. Guy stepped around the table and stood in front of Laura. "Right now, I'm just a taking a preliminary look at the ledgers to get a feel for the business and your father's bookkeeping style. For example, I noted your name on the payroll. What is it you do to earn a paycheck at the show? Sell tickets?"

Laura turned to him. A veil of sadness hung over her brown eyes. She studied his face. She started to speak, then bit at her bottom lip and blinked her eyes several times. Several tense moments passed before she answered.

"I work behind the scenes. I sew our costumes." Sadness filled Laura's whispered words.

Fighting the urge to wrinkle his brow in confusion at Laura's strange reaction to her place in the family business, Guy nodded. "I see."

"As a matter of fact, I think you're wearing some of my handiwork. Isn't that Pete's shirt?"

Guy looked down at his borrowed clothes. He and Pete shared the same clothes size but not the same physique. The stiff, rugged denim jeans and a Western-cut shirt that hung on Pete's lanky frame pulled tight across Guy's muscular legs and broad shoulders. Yet they weren't constricting. In fact, they were comfortable. But his brown wingtips looked as out of place peeking from the leg of his blue jeans as Laura did at the Wild West show in her fashionable attire.

"You're a fine seamstress." Guy smiled at Laura.

"Thanks." She flashed him a half-hearted grin. "I'm not quite the caliber of the tailor Clifford Hutton uses, but I do strive for perfection in everything I do."

"Well, it shows. Being an accomplished seamstress is a fine quality to possess." And a quality he was looking for in a wife. Guy smiled. He wanted to keep company with Laura. He was ready to settle down, and so far she had three of the qualities on his list of what he desired in a wife. She reminded him of his mother, not in looks, but in the importance of home and family. It was evident in the quality of clothes Laura provided for her brother. She took pride in running their household.

Laura's deep sigh echoed through the square room sandwiched in between the two sleeping rooms. "I hope our costumes add flare to the show. Next time we are out at the fairgrounds I'll show them to you. Speaking of showing you around, when would you like to meet Starlight?"

At the mention of her horse, Laura's eyes brightened. There was no polite way for Guy to refuse her offer. It was evident she loved her horse, a feeling Guy didn't understand or share. He turned away from her, closed his eyes and focused on keeping his breathing normal.

Visions of galloping horses ran through Guy's memories. The sound of their hooves beating the ground thundered in his ears, drowning out the rapid pace of his pulse. A large black steed reared up and towered over the other horses and a shadowy figure. Its front legs clawed at the air. Fear shivered through him.

"Afternoon and evening works best for me and Starlight. Can you adjust your schedule and fit us in?"

Guy's eyes popped open. Laura had kept talking while his memories pulled him back in time. He had no idea what she'd said. "Please forgive me. My mind wandered." He turned back and found Laura's arms crossed over her chest and her lips pursed.

"I was saying afternoons or evenings are the best time to go to the fairgrounds to visit Starlight."

"Right." Unsure if his shaking legs would hold him, Guy took a tentative step toward the davenport. "Would you join me?" He held his palm out to Laura. He hoped she'd take a seat. He wasn't certain how much longer he could remain standing.

She dropped her arms and walked, glided really, toward the blue couch. Guy closed his eyes. *Lord, please help me conquer my fears and use pleasing words to explain why I don't want a horse in the endorsements. Amen.*

In the seconds Guy spent sending up a silent prayer Laura seated herself primly on the edge of a davenport cushion. She'd turned slightly to allow for face-to-face conversation and crossed her legs at the ankle.

Guy walked around and sat at the opposite end. The worn cushion springs provided no support. Guy sank down farther than he'd anticipated. Grabbing the arm of the furniture, he adjusted his posture to match Laura's, making sure his bent knees didn't brush against hers. "It's not the best supporting piece of furniture, is it?"

"I'm afraid not. It will do for the few weeks we're in town." Laura's brown eyes locked on him.

He breathed in the faint scent of honeysuckle. Her brown eyes, round and innocent, focused on him. He leaned closer. "I don't know when I'll have the time to get out to the fairgrounds. Reviewing your show's book work is time consuming."

Her brows pulled together, moving her adorable smattering of freckles across her pert nose.

"Surely you don't plan to work all day and night for two weeks on our books." Laura's mouth formed a slight pout.

Guy hated to see even a slight unhappiness on Laura's pretty face. "No, I don't." *I plan on getting to know you better.* This was a perfect chance to ask Laura out on a date.

"So, you'll come and meet Starlight?" Laura's gaze roamed his face before her eyes locked on his. Russet highlights faceted Laura's brown eyes, giving them beautiful depth.

Lost in Laura's eyes, Guy leaned closer and nodded his head.

Small crinkles formed in the corners of Laura's eyes and she leaned toward him. There was definitely something between them. She had to feel it, too. His breath grew heavy and his eyes fluttered. A few inches closer and he'd taste her sweet lips.

The slap of her hands against her legs widened Guy's eyes. "Good. Then it's settled. Some afternoon this week, I'll take you to meet Starlight."

Chapter 5

Starlight galloped around the arena. Humidity hung thick in the morning air like webs in an abandoned barn. The August temperature blazed hot even during the midnight hours. Laura guessed it to be in the mid-seventies and it was only five-thirty in the morning. By noon time it'd be a scorcher.

Laura breathed deeply and enjoyed the cool breeze Starlight's gait created. She'd practiced her complete routine. In a standing position with her arms stretched to the sky, she took a moment to catch her breath. The view on the back of a galloping horse was incredible. Closer areas, the bleachers and nearby corn fields, passed in a blur. In the distance, where she kept her focus to help her keep her balance, she witnessed God's artistry in the vibrant oranges and reds taking small bites out of the darkness. Once the day broke, Laura's practice time ended.

Starlight's stride remained steady and straight even without Laura guiding the reins. The twelve-year-old paint deserved recognition for her part in this act, too. Laura needed to campaign hard to get Starlight included on the endorsement contract. At least one of them needed to be acknowledged.

Laura hadn't seen hide nor hair of Guy since the afternoon he'd agreed to meet Starlight three days ago. He even declined her dad's invitation to join them for worship at Cottonwood Landings church. Their show's bookkeeping wasn't so important he couldn't spare an hour to come meet Starlight. Was he avoiding her? The thought niggled at her mind.

Tired of waving to an imaginary crowd, Laura lowered her hands. Was he really avoiding her? Probably. He was an infuriating man with his strong opinions of a woman's place, yet she must endure his company until she found out all the information she'd need if she left the show. If Papa Fizzy's had scouted other trick riders as thoroughly as Guy said, he held the facts she needed to secure her future.

She started to slip back into the saddle and sighed, remembering his dreamy expression and sparkling blue eyes that took all of her resolve not to lean into. She didn't have much dating experience, but for a moment on the davenport she thought he might kiss her. Something she didn't plan to allow any man to do unless they were officially courting. It was maddening the way his kind smile melted her anger. What was wrong with her?

Laura grabbed for the reins. Overshooting the leather straps, she fisted air and lost her balance. She slid sideways. Neither foot was hooked in the special straps on her saddle, so she couldn't position her body into a riding trick. She'd shifted too far to recover her balance on her own.

She grabbed for the high saddle horn with her right hand. Making contact, she clasped her left hand over her right and threw her left leg over the saddle and the side of her horse.

"Whoa, Starlight." She bent her knees until she hung at the mare's side in a curled position. She'd made a grave mistake during the dismount of the riding trick—she had let her mind wander.

Tilting her head, she looked for the reins. They'd fallen to the other side. "Whoa, girl. Whoa, Starlight."

The muscles in her arms began to ache as they supported her weight. She looked down. The brown earth blurred. Starlight's front hooves pelted her with clumps of dirt, the sharp sting a taunting reminder of her riding mistake. If Starlight would slow her gait just a little bit, Laura might be able to push off enough that she wouldn't tumble beneath her horse's back legs.

Starlight wouldn't slow down; her horse was too well trained. It didn't matter how many times she hollered "whoa." The mare, used to her rider's shifting weight during the performance routine, wouldn't slow her pace until someone pulled on the reins.

Laura sucked in a deep breath. There was only one thing to do. Drop. Pulling her knees tight to her chest, she let go of the saddle horn with her left hand and placed it flat on the saddle. She released her breath and right hand at the same time and pushed with her left.

Gravity yanked her to the ground. Her bottom hit the hard soil of the arena first. The sharp jolt at the point of impact jarred her body, sending shock waves through her until her teeth clacked. The force bounced her to her side.

Curl into a ball. Laura tried to obey her mind's command and bent her knees, pulling them close to her body. A pinching pressure clapped against her calf. The pain slowed her reaction time. Starlight's back hoof caught the back of her leg. Luckily, she practiced in knee-length leather boots, her skin's only protection from being cut by the horse's shoe.

The dampness of the dewy soil soaked through her buckskin pants. She had a few seconds to recover before Starlight would round the arena. Lying still, her chest heaved, her breath huffed out. With a grimace, she pushed herself into a sitting position. Starlight galloped around the outside parameter of the arena, making the turn at the opposite end of the arena.

"Sis, are you all right?" Pete jumped on the fencing mid-run. One foot hit the middle fence rail to give him momentum, then he flung his legs over the top and ran toward Laura.

"I think so." Laura rubbed her boot where Starlight's hoof had met her leg. Tingles of pain still lingered. Laura knew the bone wasn't broken, but she'd sport a bruise, a trophy for her mistake.

Pete's strong arms helped lift her from the dirt. Gingerly, she tested her leg. Her calf muscle tightened and sent a complaint shooting up her leg. Wincing, she took a hobbled step. Pete held on to her while she limped across the arena to the fence.

"What happened?"

"I let my mind wander coming out of the hippodrome and missed the reins." Laura's breathing returned to normal.

"Are you sure you're okay?"

"Yeah." Laura slipped through the wide berth between the board fence rails.

"What are you doing still out here in the daylight?" Pete looked around the area.

"Practicing and thinking." Laura brushed some dust from her buckskin practice pants. Although it wasn't the full-blown Buckskin Jones outfit, it was similar. The perfect execution of a trick depended on everything, including the weight of the rider's clothing.

"Well, you'd better get back to town before someone sees you. I'll take care of Starlight."

Laura nodded and gingerly took a step, biting her lip to stifle a moan.

"Can you make the walk back to town?"

"Yes, it's exactly what this tight leg muscle needs."

By the time Laura hit the city limits of Cottonwood Landing, the town had started to come to life. She needed to get to her suite fast. She tried to quicken her pace. Even with the kink worked out of her muscle, she still limped.

The lobby of the hotel never looked more inviting than when she stepped through the door. She surveyed the large square room. The desk clerk took his breakfast during this hour of the day. No one else occupied any of the benches or chairs scattered around the lobby.

Laura started her quick hobble across the plush rose rug, dreading the flight of stairs that lay ahead of her.

"Laura?"

She stopped with her foot in mid-air over the first stair. She looked up into Guy's blue eyes. A tingle of excitement shivered through her.

"What are you doing?" He hovered two steps above her.

She smiled. "I'm going up to my suite."

The corner of Guy's mouth twitched. "That I can see.

What I meant was why are you dressed in buckskins?"
Guy's eyes roved over her. "And covered with dirt."

Laura watched his eyes retrace their previous path
over her clothing. His lips tightened. He put his fingers
under his nose.

Starlight and Laura's hard work permeated her practice clothes. She looked down at the dust-covered buckskins before looking back at Guy.

Scrutiny replaced the appreciation that had glowed
in his eyes yesterday. A flush rushed up her face. Of
all people to see her looking and smelling this way, it
had to be Guy.

"I was exercising the horses and cleaning the stalls."
She moved over a few inches and stepped up, smiling
through the pain when she put weight on her calf. It
was bad enough he saw her in this condition. He didn't
need to know she'd injured herself.

Guy's frown intensified the heat on her cheeks.

"That is too dangerous a job for a woman. Surely
your father has hired men who could exercise the horses
and muck the stalls."

Laura narrowed her eyes. Had Guy shivered when
he said the word horses? "Exactly what do you mean
by that?"

"I mean what I said. It's a man's world and young
ladies shouldn't be out trying to do a man's job. They
should be home, where it's *safe,* running the household
and raising a family."

It took her a second to realize her jaw had dropped
at his statement. She closed her mouth and pressed her
lips tight. He was worse than her father. At least her dad
believed a girl could work. *Dressed like a man.*

Maybe he wasn't worse. Hurt tornadoed through her,
spinning until it built a storm of anger in her heart. She

pursed her lips hard to keep from telling Guy what she thought of him and his opinion. She couldn't chance ruining the endorsement deal. Her family needed the money and it might be her only chance to stop the lying and perform under her own name.

Her clothes! Guy was intelligent. Would he figure out their ruse after seeing her dressed this way? She needed to get to their suite.

Fortunately, other lodgers came down the stairs just at that moment. Guy descended the last few steps. "Enjoy your breakfast." Laura called over her shoulder and nodded to the elderly couple slowly going down the stairs.

She tried to hurry. Each painful step delivered a reminder of her preoccupation with Guy's handsome features. Why was she even daydreaming about the infuriating man in the first place? Her father needed to sign the contract today and send Guy packing to the city. Laura would go back to her original plan to finish out the season dressed in buckskins and portraying a man. After she turned twenty-one if her dad didn't allow her to ride and be billed as Laura Barnes, All-American Girl, she'd find a Wild West company that would.

Gritting her teeth and grasping the handrail, Laura ascended the last step and limped down the hall to their suite. She needed to read the contract to determine the endorsement's time frame. She didn't want to get locked into years of keeping up this ruse. Obeying God's Commandment and honoring her father was getting harder and harder for her do. Besides, honoring him by keeping this deception broke another commandment.

Laura opened the door to their suite. "Dad. Dad, are you here?" She went to the door of the room he and Pete shared. The old, wooden door rattled in the frame when she knocked her knuckles hard against it.

Of course he wasn't here. He was probably in the dining room having breakfast. She turned and looked at Guy's work. An urge to rake her arm across his neatly stacked papers and perfectly aligned books shot through her, yet if she messed this up he might stay longer. Which was the last thing she wanted him to do. Her heart squeezed. Wasn't it?

Yes, it was. She'd had enough of his opinions about working women and her attire. She didn't care what he thought of her. And it was obvious she wasn't going to get any useful business information out of him.

Laura huffed over to a mirror. A chunk of her bangs stood straight up. A few strands were matted together and stuck to her forehead. Smudges of dirt created a war-paint pattern across her nose and cheeks. She swallowed hard. She couldn't believe she'd let Guy see her this way.

The force of his hurtful words filled her heart again. He shared her father's opinions, yet her dad's views annoyed her more than hurt her. Why did Guy's words cut her to the core?

She brushed moisture from her eyes, walked to the closet and pulled the strongbox off the shelf. Lifting the lid, she removed the contract.

Taking the contract to the table, she flipped the pages until she found the signature line. She'd endure another season or year of performing under the guise of Buckskin Jones if it meant Guy would go back to the city. She grabbed a pencil from Guy's work area and scanned the contract. The monetary offer was acceptable. Putting the lead to the line, she started to move the pencil. Her eyes caught the time frame of the contract.

Two years. The endorsement deal was for two years.

Laura laid the pencil down. She didn't know what was worse—performing her routine disguised as a man and letting Pete take the credit or putting up with Guy.

"Oh, that's much better." Guy stood when Laura entered the living room area of the Barneses' suite. The grackle-head blue of her simple silk crepe dress complemented her red hair. Made in the popular two-piece style, the dress had short sleeves and an embroidered net collar. The silky fabric skimmed her body and accentuated her lovely figure. She wore wool stockings instead of nylon. Although they didn't hinder her outfit in any way, they seemed like a warm choice for mid-August.

Laura's eyes darted to the elderly maid cleaning the kitchenette before her gaze met Guy's, reining his admiration of her loveliness to a halt.

Fierceness shone in her narrowed brown eyes when she glanced his way before she walked across the room to the table by the door, stepping lightly on her right leg. He'd noticed her limping across the hotel lobby on his descent down the staircase. Why Jack Barnes allowed his precious daughter around those wild beasts was beyond Guy. Her job sewing costumes was perfect and enough of a contribution to the family business.

Picking up her cloche, Laura continued to stare him down without saying a word. He caught the slight grimace on her lips with each step over to the davenport, where she sat down on the edge of a cushion. Her deft fingers quickly worked to remove the green adornment from her straw hat.

Slipping his hands in his front pockets, Guy strolled to the davenport and hovered over the back. He hoped to catch a whiff of her honeysuckle fragrance. "How clever! You designed your own removable hat band. I'm guessing you have other interchangeable adornments to match your outfits."

Laura kept her eyes on the band, clasping the hook and eye together before balancing the circle of fabric on the overstuffed arm of the couch.

Guy expected her to look up and answer, not grow more sullen. This behavior bordered on impolite. He drew a deep breath. Laura was too refined to be impolite. Perhaps she and her father had had a disagreement. When he'd found out his mother sided with Mr. Turner about Guy starting out in sales, they'd had quite a row. It had not been his finest hour honoring his mother or God's Commandment. He hadn't wanted to talk to anyone, not even God, for hours after the confrontation. Maybe something similar was bothering Laura.

He'd try another angle. "I walked to the corner and picked up a newspaper instead of going to the dining room. I thought perhaps you'd join me for breakfast."

Laura shot him a look, making him take a step backward.

"Why would I join you for breakfast? You owe me an apology."

Guy's exhale spurted from him, sounding like the pressure release after popping the cap off a bottle of Papa Fizzy's Cream Soda. What on earth was she talking about? Hadn't he just told her she looked nice when she entered the room?

The pace of his heart ticked off the silent seconds between them. Laura lacked the same enthusiasm her family seemed to have about the contract. He didn't plan to amend the contract to add the horse. Could that be what raised her dander?

"I have no idea what I've done to offend you. I beg your pardon. Please accept my apology."

Shock registered on Laura's face. "You don't know what you've done, but you're apologizing?"

Guy's eyes roamed the room. He didn't know how to defuse anger and disbelief.

"Yes." His whispered answer hissed through the room.

She rubbed her fingers across her forehead while shaking her head. After letting out a deep sigh, she looked at him. "You should at least know what you're apologizing for. You insulted me on the stairs."

Guy raised his hand to his chest. "This morning?"

"Yes, this morning." Laura pursed her lips.

It took a few moments for Guy to recreate their conversation. "Was it my shock at how dusty you were?"

He rounded the davenport and sat on the cushion beside her.

"Yes, and telling me a woman's place is in the home." Defiance flashed in Laura's brown eyes. She set her jaw. Her tightly gripped fingers scrunched the edge of her straw hat.

Guy removed the cloche from her hand and carefully placed it beside the band resting on the seat's arm. He sandwiched her right hand with his hands. Her softness, a mix of foreign and familiar, made him smile.

"I didn't mean to insult you. Some jobs aren't meant for polite ladies. I believe exercising horses is one of them." Guy hoped the sincerity he felt showed in his actions and tone of voice. He wished Laura could meet his mother. His mother ran a precise household while fulfilling many social duties. She lived the Biblical example of the wife of noble character found in *Proverbs* even after his father passed away. The same qualities

Guy sought in a wife. He knew it'd bring his mother pleasure to share her secrets with Laura.

Laura's intent stare sent anxiety rushing through Guy.

"I don't agree with you."

"You don't have to, but I believe I'm right. I saw you limping in the lobby and just now you tender-footed it across the room. You are injured, aren't you?"

A deep sigh filled the room. Laura dropped her eyes to their clasped hands. So far she hadn't tried to pull her hand free, a good sign.

She looked up at him. "Yes. I have a bad bruise. Nothing to worry about."

He knitted his brows. "Do you need to see a doctor? I can call one over."

"No, I told you it's just bruised. It's happened to me before and I'm sure it will happen to me again."

The matter-of-factness that replaced the fight in her voice irritated Guy. He needed to talk to Jack about Laura's involvement with those horses. It only took one horse to damage a person's health.

"Well, it shouldn't." Guy patted the top of her hand. "I am sorry if I offended you. It was not my intention. To show you how truly sorry I am, I'm going downstairs and ordering a tray of breakfast to be delivered to your room."

"You should probably elevate that leg." The maid's voice startled Guy. So lost in his concern for Laura, he'd forgotten she was in the room.

"That's a splendid idea." Guy released Laura's hand and stood. He grabbed the two stiff throw pillows from their placement on the davenport, fluffed them the best he could and leaned them against the furniture's arm.

Expecting that Laura would make herself comfortable, Guy strode over to the chair behind the table where he worked, grabbed his jacket and slipped it on. He turned to find Laura on her feet, staring him down.

"Mr. Roberts, I'll have you know, I'm no shrinking violet."

Chapter 6

The instant Guy's head jerked up and Laura saw hurt dulling his blue eyes, remorse pressed down on her heart stronger than the pressure of Starlight's hoof to her calf this morning. The squeezing pain in her chest felt ten times more intense than the throbbing in her leg.

She lowered her raised foot. By the sadness in Guy's eyes, her words didn't need to be emphasized by a hard stomp.

He stood, his movements frozen, his mouth agape. His suit jacket dangled off one shoulder. She'd been so defensive of his opinion of a woman's place in society, she'd missed his true intentions. He'd been showing genuine concern for her well-being. He'd tried to pamper her because of her injury. It had nothing to do with her occupation. He didn't even know she was the trick rider in her family's business.

The emotions Guy invoked confounded her. "That

didn't come out quite right. Thank you for your thoughtfulness."

With a slight wince, she stepped around the coffee table. She wished she could come clean and tell him the truth. This type of injury came with the territory, but the truth would jeopardize the endorsement offer. Guy wanted a male trick rider to endorse their soda pop, and their show needed the extra cash. So did Laura. She couldn't forget why he was here.

Laura swallowed her disdain of his opinion and the likely correct assumption that she should rest her leg. "I planned to walk to the bakery for a light breakfast. They make the most delicious cinnamon rolls. Would you care to join me?"

She intended to flash Guy a wide smile to let him know all was forgiven. Her emotions thought otherwise. The tom-tom drum of her heart switched from nervous that he'd join her to anxious that he wouldn't with each beat. Her lips twitched into a tentative smile.

Blinking twice and straightening his shoulders, Guy nodded. He pushed his other arm through his jacket, adjusted the lapel, and began to button the double-breasted front.

"Somehow, we seem to misunderstand each other." Guy stepped toward her with a cocked elbow. "Let's try to work through that today, shall we?"

Guy's warm smile and the yearning in his eyes melted Laura's heart.

"I'd planned to ask you to accompany me on a shopping excursion in downtown Cottonwood Landing. I failed to pack for a two-week stay." The corners of Guy's lips turned down, changing his bright smile into a frown. "I can't keep borrowing Pete's clothing. If you have no obligations, I'd be pleased if you'd join me."

Guy's brow furrowed. "Or is shopping too much of a strain on your leg?"

Her heart cantered at his concern. "I believe it's just what my leg needs." Laura grabbed her cloche and slipped it over her head, then looped her arm through Guy's.

Guy insisted on driving the few short blocks to Cottonwood Landing's Main Street, which didn't allow any time for Laura to initiate a conversation about what Papa Fizzy's learned concerning women trick riders and their earnings.

Parking in front of the bakery, Guy turned off the car engine. Laura reached for the door handle.

"Allow me." Guy's light touch on her arm stopped her motion.

"But I can manage."

"I know." Firmness settled on Guy's handsome face. "A gentleman doesn't allow a lady to open her own door."

Stifling the urge to do the contrary of what Guy asked, Laura placed both hands in her lap. This was her perfect opportunity to ask Guy questions and learn the truth about the way the world treated women performers.

"Better." Guy gave her a curt nod and smiled.

Laura watched Guy round the front of the car. Giddy anticipation fluttered through her. No one had ever opened a car door for her. This must be what a real date felt like.

The click of the door latch releasing pulled her back into the moment. This wasn't a date. It was a business meeting. When she turned to get out of the car, her calf brushed the seat. A sharp pain shot up her leg, a reminder that she needed to keep her focus.

The homey scent of fresh-baked bread welcomed them when they entered the bakery. While Guy placed their order, Laura waited by a long wooden counter on one side of the wall where customers stood enjoying their sweet treats instead of sitting at tables. Laura balanced most of her weight on one leg to relieve the pressure on her injured calf.

Guy and Laura visited with the baker while they savored their warm cinnamon rolls and ice-cold glasses of milk.

"Shall we get started?"

Aggravation laced through Laura. She was never going to get a chance to question Guy.

"Thank you again for breakfast." Laura limped the first few steps to the door.

"It was my pleasure." Guy opened the heavy wood door, allowing Laura to pass over the threshold before he followed her out to the sidewalk.

The air inside the bakery had been stale and warm but nothing like the oppressive humidity mixed with the heat of the day; even standing in the shade of the awning covering the bakery's large plate-glass window provided little relief. Guy removed the handkerchief from his jacket pocket and mopped his brow.

"The large fan we sat in front of spoiled me."

"Why don't you put your jacket in the car and roll up your shirt sleeves?" Laura knew his dark suit magnified the warmth of the sun.

"I'll manage. Where is the department store?"

Main Street stretched for three blocks and was composed of various-size buildings. Each block had a few stately rust-red brick, two-story buildings housing banks and attorney offices. The doctor's office, hardware store and most of the other buildings were one story with false facades to give them height. The bakery and the five-and-dime sat on opposite sides of the street in the center of the second block of downtown.

"You have two to choose from and they are at opposite ends of the downtown. I learned the Montgomery Ward opened here last year." Laura pointed toward a building a block away. "Bell's is a family-owned variety store. It's one block down on this side of the street."

"In honor of our family businesses, I'll try Bell's first." He offered his arm to Laura.

She reached her hand out, then stopped. She looked up and down the street. Although there was little traffic in town and the number of shoppers were a few, she couldn't chance one of their employees reporting back to her father that they'd seen her arm in arm with a man downtown. "It's not proper. My father wouldn't approve."

"Okay." Guy didn't hide his disappointment when he lowered his arm. He stepped around Laura so he could walk on the curb side of the street. "It is refreshing to find a girl who honors her father's wishes." Guy's blue eyes twinkled when his gaze met hers. "It's a pleasing attribute."

The light airy cinnamon roll instantly turned to lead in her stomach. Her outward appearance showed she honored her father's wishes. Her thoughts didn't always prove that to be true. She knew God wanted her thoughts and actions to honor her father. She shouldn't be scheming behind his back. She needed to spend more time in prayer giving this situation to God and letting Him sort it out.

"Did I say something wrong?"

"Oh, no." Laura glanced at Guy. "I was lost in thought."

They paused at the corner while a rusty truck sputtered through the intersection. Awkward silence hung heavier than the humidity in the air around them. Guy swung his arms in front of him, snapping one fisted hand into the open palm of the other.

As they crossed the street, Laura wondered why she had agreed to accompany Guy. She wanted to be around him, but then when she was, she couldn't think of a thing to say.

"Does the show set up in this area yearly?" Guy stuffed his hands in his pockets.

"About every other year. We've found we draw bigger crowds that way." Laura found taking shorter steps helped with the pain in her leg.

"Absence makes the heart grow fonder?" Guy realized he was a few steps ahead of Laura when he turned. He stopped. "We should have taken the car."

"Nonsense. I can walk a block and half." Laura looked over her shoulder at Guy's shiny car parked in front of the bakery.

They finally reached the broad windows of Bell's department store. Mannequins welcomed them with big smiles and the latest summer fashions. A large ventilator fan whirred above the door, cutting through their silence like the blades slashed the humid air.

"Good morning," a woman said from behind a silver cash register and long wooden counter.

"How may I help you today?"

"I'm looking for some casual clothing. Could you point me in the direction of your men's department?"

"Certainly. It's right this way." The woman started walking toward a back corner of the store.

A sheepishness crept into Guy's features. "I'd welcome your opinion on my selections but I don't believe it's proper for you to accompany me to the men's department."

Guy's concern for her reputation warmed Laura's heart and brought a soft smile to her lips. "I'll just look around while you make your choices."

Laura waved Guy off with her fingers. She moved to the ladies' clothing, noting styles and colors of the popular items placed on display. She liked several and knew she could make easy alterations to the patterns she already owned.

Heading to the notions department to peruse their offerings Laura walked by the shoe department. She caught her breath.

A pair of bright red cowboy boots sat on an end display. They were a perfect match to her red leather riding skirt and vest she'd made and hidden in the back of her closet along with the white satin blouse.

The low, almost nonexistent, heels of the boots would aid her in keeping her balance while standing on Starlight's back. She'd lengthened the legs of the riding skirt so the split skirt's hem grazed her leg right below her knee. With the bloomer panel she'd sewed into the skirt and the knee-high boot shaft, she'd show very little of her uncovered leg. Her dad couldn't disapprove of this outfit. It was anything but risqué with no chance of ruining her reputation.

Lifting the boot, she looked at the price and cringed. If she purchased them, it would put a dent in her savings, but it'd be an investment in her future. Laura slid her hand into the side pocket of her dress and fingered the dollar she'd put in to cover her breakfast at the bakery. Now she was glad Guy had insisted on paying for their rolls and milk. Perhaps the store would hold the boots for her if she gave them this dollar and promised to return before they closed for the day to pay the remainder and pick up the boots.

Laura craned her neck, searching the store for another clerk. She'd wanted to try on the boots and hoped they stocked her size. The scuff of a heel on the wooden floorboards behind her brought a smile to her lips. She started to turn.

"Woo wee, those are fancy boots."

Panic shot through her, doubling her heart's pace. Of all people to catch her looking at the boots, why did it have to be Clifford? Her heart pitched a fit in her chest. If he figured out their ruse, he'd waste no time spreading the word of their lie. Another good reason why her dad should ditch the character and let her perform as an all-American girl. That type of billing couldn't hurt her reputation.

"Good morning, Laura." Clifford stood uncomfortably close to her and lifted the boot from her hand. He let out a low whistle. "These are something, aren't they?"

"Good morning, Clifford. They are very eye-catching." Panic edged her voice. She prayed that self-centered Clifford didn't hear it.

"I'll say. The intricate stitching and the big cut-out star pattern here in the middle are pretty." Clifford pointed to the embellishment like Laura had missed it. "Kind of matches those stars on Starlight's bridle harness, doesn't it?"

Laura caught her surprise in her throat and almost choked. The fancy work was another reason she felt they were perfect for her act. She'd adorned the sides of her riding skirt and vest with white stars. "I...um...never thought about that." She widened her eyes and tried to fix an innocent expression on her face.

"Really?" Clifford quirked a brow. "They'd make a big splash with a crowd."

"You would know." Laura looked Clifford up and down. His attire today was toned down to sensible leather boots and brown denim pants. The yoke of his Western-cut shirt was a light green, which matched the brown and green plaid of the shirt's body and sleeves. The shirt had brown buttons instead of his usual pearl snaps.

He pushed his straw cowboy hat back on his head, freeing blond curls to hang across his forehead. "Yes, I would. A professional performer has to look and dress the part at all times."

"Excuse me, miss. The gentleman is requesting you come to see the clothing he's chosen." The sales clerk smiled at Laura, then turned her attention to Clifford. "Are you interested in those boots?"

"No, ma'am, but I believe this little filly is." Clifford exaggerated a wink at Laura, sending a chill through her. Did he know what she was up to? Impossible, yet doubt niggled at her mind every time she had a conversation with him.

Laura took the boot from Clifford and returned it to the display shelf. She flashed a polite smile at the sales clerk. "They are very attractive. I was just looking. Please show me the way to Mr. Roberts."

"You're shopping with the dude from the city?"

Laura's shoulders sagged. "Mr. Roberts is a business associate. His stay was extended and he needed to purchase additional clothing. I came along to keep him company."

"I'm sure you did."

In answer to Clifford's raised eyebrows Laura turned and followed the clerk to the men's department.

"Oh!" Laura put a hand to her throat. She'd expected to see Guy in a suit made of seersucker or linen to help him endure the summer heat.

He turned from the mirror. "You don't approve?"

"Oh, I approve. I'm just surprised at your choice." A cobalt-blue Western-cut shirt, that matched his beautiful eyes, stretched across his broad shoulders. Dark denim jeans cinched with a black belt led down to square-toed black boots. The transformation from stuffy business-man to a cowboy suited him. "You look very hand-some."

The happiness dancing in Guy's eyes at her compliment pulled instant heat to her cheeks and widened her smile.

Their gazes locked. She delighted in the appreciation shining from Guy's eyes. She knew it wasn't proper to allow a man to look at her in this way in a public place, especially with a sales clerk and Clifford looking on, but she refused to break their stare, knowing full well her brown eyes reflected the same shining light Guy's blue eyes did. The thrill shooting through her was more exhilarating than the roaring crowd's applause after her perfect execution of the back drag.

Not until she heard Clifford's snort and retreating footsteps thundering on the wooden floorboards of the store did Laura look down. She bit her lip. *Dear God, please don't let him go tell Father.*

Guy fought the urge to hit his palm against the hard metal of the steering wheel. Just when things were meshing between him and Laura, that rogue Clifford had to show up. After he made a spectacle stomping out of the store, Laura's eyes dulled with an emotion nothing short of fear.

Although she visited with the sales clerk while Guy changed back into his suit, he couldn't even get her to make polite conversation on the ride back to the hotel. It was obvious Clifford Hutton liked Laura. He puffed and strutted in his bright-colored clothing like a peacock fanning its feathers to attract a mate.

Laura didn't seem to return his interest, or at least not in Guy's presence. So why did Clifford's departure rattle her so?

The few minutes it took to drive from Main Street to the hotel seemed like hours in the dead silence between them. Guy eased his Durant Star alongside the picket fence separating the hotel grounds from the street. "What are you looking for?

Laura had been ducking her head and glancing from the windshield to the side window since the two-story square frame came into view.

"What?"

She turned to Guy. He knew she didn't really see him. She tilted her head, looking past him at the opposite side of the street.

"I asked you what you were looking for."

Laura's eyes found his. "Clifford's truck."

"I see." Guy's words clipped out.

Laura placed her hand on his arm. "No, you don't. My dad doesn't let me date without his approval. Clifford's asked several times only to receive no for an answer. I think he may have gotten the wrong impression about our shopping trip today and…"

"You're afraid he's trying to find your father?"

Regret pinched Laura's features. "Yes, yes, that's it."

Guy patted Laura's soft hand still resting on his forearm. "I won't let Clifford make any trouble. I'll explain the situation to your father. After all, we are on the verge of becoming business partners. There will be times we are seen together."

Laura smiled at his explanation, but it was tinged with sadness. She pulled her hand away from his arm. He took the cue to slip from the car, round the front and open the car door for her.

"How's your leg?"

"It's sore. I think the walking helped loosen up the muscle, though."

Laura waited beside the gate while Guy retrieved his purchases, which were wrapped in brown paper and tied with a string.

They strolled up the narrow cement walkway to the hotel. A covered porch stretched the entire front of the structure. An intricately carved railing, painted white, lined the edge of the porch. A swing hung at one end. Brown wicker furniture arranged for easy conversation sat on the other end of the porch shaded by a cottonwood tree.

Guy caught Laura's slight wince when she stepped on the first stair. Clasping her elbow for extra support, he assisted her with the remaining five stairs. He stepped quickly and opened the screen door wide as booming laughter filled the space. His heart jumped to his throat. Even Clifford's laugh drawled.

Laura lowered her eyes and shook her head. Her reaction confirmed that the other man's voice belonged to her dad, Jack Barnes.

"Don't worry," Guy whispered into her ear when she stepped past him over the threshold. "I'll speak to your father."

"Where're your new duds?" Clifford locked his gaze on Guy.

Clifford's question didn't dignify a verbal response.

Lifting the parcels, Guy met Clifford's stare. Laura stood close to her father with her eyes riveted to the roses on the plush area rug. Clifford might rattle a gentle young woman, but he didn't intimidate Guy.

"Mr. Barnes, I hope you don't mind. Since Laura is familiar with the area I asked her to accompany me downtown this morning to choose more appropriate attire for my extended stay."

With a flex of his shoulders and a slight purse to his lips, Jack sent a shiver of intimidation through Guy. Holding himself ramrod straight, he stood three inches shorter than Jack, but the urge to protect and defend Laura made him feel six inches taller. "I assure you, sir, it was an innocent shopping trip. I'd never do anything to tarnish Laura's reputation."

Clifford's soft chuckle spurred Guy on. "As a matter of fact, I'm seeking your permission to take Laura out on a date tomorrow."

Laura lost interest in the rug and raised widened eyes to Guy.

"That is if Laura is agreeable." Guy's words rushed from him.

Clifford threw his head back. His guffaws echoed off the pressed tin ceiling. He missed seeing Laura turn to her father and give a slight nod.

Jack Barnes crossed his arms over his chest and narrowed his eyes at Guy. His actions drew another round of laughter from Clifford. Clifford clapped Guy on the back so hard, his body jerked forward. "City slicker, you have a lot to learn."

Raising his brows, Jack gave Clifford a disgusted look, then rubbed his chin and looked back at Guy. "It's okay with me if it's okay with Laura."

Chapter 7

Laura pinched her lips tight to keep her mouth from gaping. She watched her father walk across the lobby of the hotel and pick up a newspaper. Had he really said it was up to her if she wanted to go on a date with Guy? Or had the dull ache in her calf clouded her mind like the humidity fogged the late-morning air.

"Well, Laura? Shall we spend the afternoon in the park and stop for ice cream at the soda fountain in the drugstore?" A trickle of sweat zigzagged down the side of Guy's face.

Clifford might not intimidate Guy, but her father did. Guy proved braver than many of the tough cowboys who tried to talk her into sneaking away for a date rather than asking her father for permission.

Though Laura didn't agree with all of Guy's opinions, he did have admirable qualities. Besides, a date was the perfect opportunity to talk to him about business.

"That sounds very nice." Laura nodded.

Her heart kicked and bucked with happiness. The same glint shined from his eyes as earlier in the day. His glistening blue eyes captivated her, made it hard for her to look away.

For a few seconds Guy held their gaze, then he looked at Clifford. Happiness etched Guy's features. He flashed a smug smile toward Clifford.

Clifford returned his smile with a warning glare before he looked at Laura and quirked his brow. "Maybe you should go horseback riding instead."

"I don't believe Guy knows how to ride." Although wariness washed through her, Laura tried to inflect innocence in her answer.

"Is that so?" Clifford slid his hat back on his head. "Laura's an excellent rider. I'm sure she could teach you a few tricks."

Clifford's stare bored into Laura. Her stomach lurched. Did he know?

Rejoining the group, her father gave Clifford a playful swat on the back with the newspaper. "Got time for a cup of coffee? Mr. Roberts has offered Buckskin Jones an endorsement contract. Since you're always trying to get an endorsement, I thought maybe you could answer some questions for us."

Anxiety bubbled through every inch of Laura's body. She didn't want Clifford to join them. His knowing looks may be a bluff, but they made her uncomfortable. Yet this meeting could provide the information she needed to persuade her dad to give her the top billing.

"I've got nothing but time. How about you, city boy?"

"I'll join you after I give my parcels to the front desk clerk." Guy stepped toward the oak counter.

"After you, Laura." Clifford tipped his hat and made an exaggerated bow.

Laura stepped in front of him, following close behind her dad to avoid any more of Clifford's comments.

Her father chose a corner table at the far end of the restaurant and waited for Laura to be seated. She hesitated a few seconds, trying to buy time for Guy to join them. She knew if she sat, both men present would flank her, leaving Guy to be seated across from her instead of beside her. Then again, maybe that would be best. She could angle her body away from Clifford to avoid his pointed looks.

The waitress left with their beverage order as Guy walked up to the table and sat in the empty chair.

"Clifford, Mr. Roberts offered an endorsement deal to Buckskin Jones."

"Excuse me, sir," Guy interrupted. "Pete Barnes. We offered the endorsement deal to Pete Barnes."

Laura puckered her lips at Guy's correction.

"Shouldn't he be here if we are going to talk about the contract?"

Laura's father shook his head. "We're not going to talk about the specifics of our contract. I plan to ask Clifford if he can verify what you told us."

"About a woman trick rider, specifically Winona Phelps, making twice the amount you offered us, since a woman doing death-defying stunts on horseback provides bigger thrills." Laura's words rushed out in one long breath. She turned to Clifford. "Do you know if this is true?"

Clifford puckered his brows and pinched all his features together, exaggerating his depth of thought. "I heard she signed a two-year contract with a candy bar company for around three thousand dollars. Guess I don't know if it's double what Roberts offered you."

"Three thousand dollars!" Laura couldn't contain her astonishment. The figure *was* twice the amount Papa Fizzy's had offered Pete and matched the information in the articles Laura had read.

The waitress set four coffees on the table.

Her father lifted his cup, blew across it and took a small sip. "Are you telling the honest truth, Clifford?"

"Yes, sir, I am." Clifford lifted his fingers in the Boy Scouts honor sign. "Although I don't have an endorsement deal, I do know other Roman riders and male trick riders who endorse products. They don't get near that amount, and their contracts span a longer period of time."

Laura shot her dad a pointed look. He briefly made eye contact with her and crossed his arms over his chest.

"Why do you think that is?"

"Crowds get a bigger kick out of a pretty girl in a fancy outfit doing riding tricks."

Laura felt Clifford's stare boring down on her. It took all of her effort not to look his way.

"See Mr. Barnes, our research is accurate. Papa Fizzy's offer is in alignment with other endorsement offers to male performers in rodeos and Wild West shows. Are you ready to sign the contract now?" Guy lifted his cup to his lips.

"No." Laura hadn't meant to give voice to her thought. "I mean, we need to discuss this with Pete and there's still the matter of adding Starlight to the contract."

Guy looked at Laura. The color drained from his

face. The hand holding his cup trembled, and coffee splashed over the edge.

"Even though you don't ride, perhaps if we have time tomorrow afternoon, we can go to the fairgrounds so you can meet Starlight. Now that you have more casual attire, I could give you a riding lesson if you'd like."

Using both hands, Guy set his coffee cup on the table. His Adam's apple bounced in a hard swallow. "I thought we had come to an agreement about the horse."

"I told you her name is Starlight, not 'the horse,' and we haven't come to any agreement, have we Dad?"

Laura hoped her dad recognized the pleading in her voice. Maybe knowing the dollar amount of Winona's endorsement would make him drop the Buckskin Jones character. Double the money would certainly help the show.

Then she looked at Guy and remembered he didn't want a woman trick rider to endorse Papa Fizzy's Cream Soda. Disappointment threatened to droop her shoulders. She almost gave in to it until she remembered who sat to her left. A quick side glance confirmed her suspicion. Clifford's eyes were on her, and he was watching her every move. She drew her shoulders tight and placed her hands in her lap in an effort to hide her frustration from Clifford.

"Well, Roberts, if this endorsement deal doesn't work out with Pete Barnes, I'd be willing to consider putting *my* name behind your product. After all, if you do any color ads, my costumes are brighter and more eye-catching than the buckskin suit Pete wears." Clifford pushed the brim of his cowboy hat back a few inches. "And I don't want to share the spotlight with my horses. The ad should be me in a flashy Western shirt holding a bottle of your soda pop or maybe even taking a swig."

Guy's eyes rounded. "Really?"

Laura felt her own eyes grow wide. Had Cliff just swooped in on their deal? Was Guy flashing him a genuine smile?

The pulsing of her heartbeat in her ears dimmed the men's words. She looked at her father. Wasn't he going to say something? Clifford was jeopardizing their deal, the one thing that could make her dream of headlining their Wild West show come true. "Dad?"

The shrug she received for an answer ignited her temper. Her throbbing heart intensified the thundering in her ears and loosened her tongue. She turned to Guy and Clifford. "You have some nerve, Clifford Hutton, trying to steal our endorsement deal."

Guy and Clifford stopped talking. Laura's cheeks blazed under the scrutiny of Guy's stare.

"Dad, you aren't going to stand for this, are you?"

"Laura, this is business you wouldn't understand." The softness in Guy's eyes matched the tone of his voice. What was meant to tame her anger made it grow fiercer, like the frantic bucking of a wild horse experiencing the weight of a saddle for the first time.

"I do too understand. He's stealing our contract. You can't seriously consider Clifford." Laura threw her arms in the air.

"Our contract?"

Even in her anger she heard the hidden question in Clifford's voice.

"Pete's contract." Her words hissed through clenched teeth. "But it benefits the entire family."

"Laura, you aren't acting very ladylike." Her father's deep baritone smothered the flames of her anger like cold coffee thrown on a campfire.

The stern look he shot her amplified his warning

words. Stating her opinion wouldn't tarnish her reputation. She knew right from wrong. She tried not to disobey her father, but this was unjust. Cliff wanted to steal her contract, her only leverage to drop the ruse and perform under her own name.

Laura bit at her lip. Wanting to use Papa Fizzy's endorsement deal as leverage against her father wasn't honoring him in the way God had intended. Moisture sprang to her eyes. She needed to talk to her dad, show him her outfit, prove to him she could still keep her reputation intact and be the headliner in the Wild West show.

Although her anger smoldered, she put silk into her voice. "Gentleman, I'm sorry for my outburst. However, this doesn't seem like a polite thing to discuss unless we have refused the contract."

"No need to apologize, Laura." Guy's kind smile returned. "There is no way for you to know the finer details of business."

A flame sparked from the smoldering embers of Laura's anger. She pursed her lips tighter.

"Yes, maybe you'd be happier making another trip downtown to Bell's to do a little shopping for yourself, maybe for some footwear?"

It took all of her resolve to not look at Clifford.

Pulling his brows in confusion, Guy cast a sideways glance at Clifford before affixing his gaze to hers. "You see, Clifford is actually being aboveboard broaching the subject in front of your father."

Stop talking to me like I'm an idiot. Her mind spat the words she longed to say. Why had she agreed to a date with Guy? One appreciative look making her feel like the only girl in the world had derailed her. It wouldn't happen again. Tomorrow afternoon, she'd get the information she needed and never give Guy Roberts a second thought.

"Guy's right. Clifford could have sneaked around behind our backs."

Laura glared at her father. Wasn't the Barnes family sneaking around other people's backs with this little stunt of theirs?

"Besides, Laura—" Clifford waited until she turned his way "—performers have to keep their options open."

His wink and sideways grin dropped Laura's heart. Dread trotted through her like a horse heading for a haystack. Fear rounded her eyes. *He knows I'm Buckskin Jones.*

Chapter 8

"Laura, are you feeling all right?" Laura's head snapped up. The concern swimming in Guy's eyes increased the already frenzied pace of her heart. He started to rise from his chair. "You are ghost white. Is it your…"

"No!" She didn't want to make eye contact with her dad or Clifford. The weight of all the men's gazes rested on her shoulders, adding to the burden of her trick-riding secret. If Guy mentioned her injury it might be the loose thread that unraveled the family's cover-up.

Guy stood and walked around the table. "Discussing business is too much for a delicate lady. You should be upstairs resting." He guided her chair back to allow her to stand.

She remained firmly planted on the seat of the chair. She couldn't go upstairs and let Clifford steal the endorsement contract out from under them. "I'm fine. I really want to stay."

"This is too much for you. Let me escort you to your room. Jack, don't you feel Laura should get some rest?"

"Well, you do look a little pale, Laura."

Laura looked at her father. *How would you know?* His expression held concern, but it was directed at Guy, not her.

The scrape of her father's chair across the wooden floor vibrated through the room. He stood. "I was going to head to our suite. I'll make sure Laura arrives there safely and rests." He pushed past Guy and waited for Laura to stand.

"Mr. Roberts, you'll have to postpone any book work you planned to do today."

"Of course. I wouldn't want to disturb Laura. I've been telling her all morning…"

"I'm fine, really." Laura jumped from her chair, knocking the backs of her knees against the seat. The chair tilted backward.

Guy caught it before it fell.

Her father took her by the hand. "Let's go."

She winced with every step, trying to keep up with her father's stride. He stopped at the door and turned. Laura chanced a look at the two men left behind in her father's dust. Amusement danced on Clifford's features, while worry lined Guy's face. His distress over her well-being made her want to run to him and seek comfort in his arms.

Laura shook her head. What was wrong with her? How could she want to rush to his arms when just minutes ago he'd dismissed her from the business conversation? Laura's thoughts caused her heart to squeeze tight. She had to stop letting her heart cloud her thinking. Laura didn't need Guy for comfort. She needed him for his information.

"Since you won't be working on the bookkeeping, Guy, you can accompany me to the fairgrounds. We have an open spot in the show to fill. Clifford and a couple other acts are going to audition for it this afternoon. I'm sure you'll be interested in watching in case you want to offer another act an endorsement in the future."

"I don't think that's necessary." The pallet of color on Guy's cheeks changed from rosy to a deep crimson flush to stark white.

"Of course it is. You could use some fresh air. Meet me in the lobby at two this afternoon."

Without warning her father started walking. His momentum pulled her with him and she stumbled through the door.

"Dad, slow down. I fell this morning during practice and Starlight clipped my calf." She whispered her words through gritted teeth.

Her father slowed his steps. "I'm sorry, Laura. Pete told me earlier this morning. It slipped my mind. How bad is it?"

"I have a bruise about the circumference of a saddle-soap tin where her hoof caught me." Laura reached for the stair rail and her dad let go of her hand. He followed close behind as she gingerly ascended the stairs.

"Do I need to have a doctor come by and take a look?"

"I don't think so." Laura leaned against the wide oak door frame and waited for her father to unlock their suite.

Once inside, she limped to the davenport.

"Laura, I'm sorry I was walking so fast and caused you discomfort. I don't appreciate the way those two downstairs look at you. Clifford treats you like a tart, winking and smirking. Guy acts like you're a fine piece of china in danger of breaking into shards. Neither of those are the kind of girl I raised."

Drawing a deep breath, Laura's heart settled into the comfortable cradle of her father's love and protectiveness. "No, it's not." She leaned back against the furniture arm and lifted her legs to the cushions. Her dad fluffed the throw pillows and tucked them under her feet to elevate them, then perched on the opposite arm of the davenport.

"Pete said you fell dismounting from the hippodrome. You've known how to execute the stance since you were twelve. What happened? You never fall."

"I let my mind wander."

"To the endorsement contract?"

She knew better than to tell her dad she'd been daydreaming of Guy and the way her heart reeled when he looked at her. She also realized this was an opportunity to discuss her future with her father. "Yes. Dad, I don't want to portray a male character anymore. I want to be billed as Laura Barnes, the All-American Girl."

"You know how I feel about making you the star of the show. Photographers will snap pictures of you in provocative poses with alluring eyes. Men and women will think you're *that* girl. You'll develop a bad reputation the same way other women in Western show acts have."

"Those things only happen if they allow it. Crediting the act to me won't change my view or actions. I won't abandon my morals."

Sadness veiled her dad's eyes. He shook his head. "I won't have other people thinking badly of my daughter."

"Dad, we can't control other's thoughts. It isn't fair to me to do all of the work and let Pete take the credit."

"It's a man's world, Laura. When women start doing men's jobs, they jeopardize their reputations. One flippant remark can tarnish their moral character and change the course of their lives forever. I've seen it."

Laura had seen it, too. Winona Phelps became bawdy when her career star started to rise, but Laura had no desire to visit billiard rooms or see what lay behind the flash of the neon signs. She had no desire to be a flapper; she just wanted to thrill spectators with her routine and visit with them afterward.

"Nothing about me would change."

"I think it would, especially with this endorsement offer. You're a pretty and innocent girl. Some unscrupulous business manager would see the advertisement and swoop down on you like a hawk on a bunny."

Rubbing her hands over her eyes, Laura contained her sigh. It was futile to continue her plea now. She'd wait until she had a chance to speak with Guy and find out about business managers and any other information Papa Fizzy's ran across by researching acts to endorse their product. Her father had done such a fine job of raising her and Pete after their mother's death. Why couldn't he loosen the reins enough so she could prove it to him and make him proud?

"Are you certain you don't need a doctor?"

She shook her head. "I've been bruised before." *Inside and out.* Hurt yanked at her heart, twisting it until it felt tighter than the honda knot on Pete's lariat. The visible bruises healed faster than those on her heart. Moisture brimmed in her eyes.

Three months. Only three months until her twenty-first birthday. If she wanted to appear in the beautiful costume she made under her own name, she'd have to look for another show. Maybe even travel the rodeo circuit competing for prizes the same way Winona had gotten her start. Her heart squeezed. She really didn't want to work for anyone else. She loved working with her family, but her father's stubborn refusal to drop the Buckskin Jones act may deem it necessary.

"Okay, well, I'm going to go round up Guy and head to the fairgrounds. I'll see you at suppertime."

Once the door clicked closed, Laura bowed her head. Hurt trickled down her cheeks and dropped onto her folded hands. She focused her thoughts on God, the only one who could heal her bruised heart.

"What are you looking for?"

Jack Barnes booming baritone echoed through the vacant pasture and gave Guy a start.

"Just taking in the scenery." Sweat trickled down Guy's back. Fear had kick-started his heart the moment he and Jack stepped outside of the hotel door. The shakiness in his legs made it hard to keep up with Jack's stride.

The breeze wafted the nauseous scent of horse through the air, lifting and spinning the bitter aroma around him. How could he know which area to avoid if he couldn't tell the direction the smell came from? He dropped a few steps behind Jack and craned his neck, trying to catch a glimpse of the ferocious beasts. He didn't want to startle one. He'd been witness to that once in his life. The memory wrenched his stomach.

Guy looked from side to side and then forward. Jack had directed Guy to another entryway into the fairgrounds. He'd parked his car under a cottonwood tree alongside several pickups with horse trailers attached or wooden framework built up the sides of the truck box. Sweat beaded his upper lip. He knew they were near the horses.

By the time they reached the arena, nerves roiled Guy's stomach. A few men leaned over the fencing, their arms resting on the rails. Many of the show's hands wore feed caps, overalls and chambray shirts instead of traditional Western wear. Women and children dotted the benches of the bleachers.

The hands greeted their boss by name and Guy with a curt nod.

Jack placed his boot on the bottom fence rail and, in one quick move, swung his leg over the top rail, straddling the fence. "Come on up. This is the best place to watch the auditions."

Dizziness washed through Guy. No way was he putting himself in such a dangerous position. How he wished they'd sign or refuse the endorsement contract! Now Clifford had confirmed the information that Pete wanted to verify. The Barnes family knew Papa Fizzy's endorsement offer was fair. Guy planned to speak with Pete, but the boy's presence in the hotel suite was scarce compared to Jack and Laura's.

"I believe I'll watch from the top of the riser."

With a raise of his brows, Jack shrugged. "Suit yourself."

Before Guy could answer, someone called Jack's name and he turned his attention to the far arena gate.

Guy gulped. Two white horses were tethered to the fencing near the gate. Fighting the urge to run to the safety of the bleachers, Guy allowed himself to take short, quick steps until he reached the wooden benches. He saw the scrutiny on the faces of the women he passed on his way up the bleachers. He nodded curtly and con-

tinued to the top bench, certain a horse couldn't climb
the wooden seats.

He eased into a seated position. Nerves bounced his
legs, vibrating the footrest board. This is not how he
wanted to spend his afternoon. He'd rather be pouring over the Western show ledgers in the safety of the
hotel suite. The pungency of the worn leather-bound ac-
count books and the coarse paper filled with neat and
orderly numbers made sense and comforted him. Guy
just didn't understand the appeal of this, yet many people, including his mother, delighted in the life Western
movies portrayed.

Shrill whoops from the children scattered on the
bleachers drew him from his thoughts. Two white
horses, identical in size, galloped into the arena side
by side. Guy's heart jumped to his throat. Clifford stood
with one foot on each of the horses' backs. His knees
were bent and worked like shock absorbers with each
synchronized step the horses took. Holding the reins
with one hand, Clifford lifted his white cowboy hat and
waved it at the small crowd while the horses galloped
past the bleachers.

The royal-blue blankets under the black saddles with
silver conches matched Clifford's royal-blue slacks and
the yoke of his Western shirt. The remainder of his shirt
was white, coordinating with his cowboy hat and boots.
The conches adorned the saddles and also dangled from
leather straps, jingle-jangling with each movement of
the horses.

Guy sat forward, drawn in by Clifford's skill at guiding the horses while replacing his hat. The horses continued to trot around the fence line of the arena. Clifford
stepped to the back of one horse and then, with very
little effort, proceeded to hop from horse to horse.

After the small crowd cheered, he placed a foot on each horse. Without breaking their stride, the horses parted about two feet. Guy caught his breath. Clifford was going to fall. Guy stood. His heart thundered. He knew what happened when horse's hooves met a human body.

Guy gasped. Clifford remained upright with his legs spread apart. The small group clapped when he passed by them. Guy put a hand to his heart, realizing it beat with exhilaration and not fear. He sat back down on the hard board seat, scooting to the edge, anticipating Clifford's next move.

As the horses rounded the bend of the arena, Clifford slowed them. He pulled and twisted the reins, changing the sway of his body on the horses' backs. The horses began to prance, lifting their front legs high in the air.

He stopped his team in front of the bleachers and clicked his tongue, and the horses backed up.

With a quick twist, Clifford turned around on the horses and they took off running. He was riding the horses backward, yet the horses still made the turn in the arena. Amazing! Guy clapped his hands when Clifford turned around to face forward.

Clifford slowed the horses, guiding the team to the center of the arena. Without warning the horses reared up, their front legs flailing through the air. Guy's breath caught. The scene before him changed to the past. The vision of a huge black steed reared up, bringing its hooves down.

He closed his eyes and bent his head. *Please God, don't make me witness this again.*

The beat of his pulse thundered in his ears louder than the applause around him. He blinked. They were applauding. Slowly raising his head, he peeked through slit eyelids. Clifford stood between his two steeds. At his whip's signal, the horses bent their front legs and bowed their heads to the crowd.

Guy jumped to his feet and joined the small crowd's applause. His heart was racing and his breath came in pants, thrilled by Clifford's skills with his horses.

"If you think that's a good act, you should watch Buckskin Jones."

Laura stood beside him on the bleachers, her hand shading her eyes from the sun.

"Forgive me. I was so intent watching Clifford's performance, I didn't even see you climb the bleachers." Guy held his hand out to assist Laura as she stepped up on the boards to sit by him.

"I noticed."

Her curt answer caught Guy off-guard. "You don't think Clifford is a skilled horseman."

Laura's shoulders raised with a deep inhale, then lowered when she released her breath in a huff. "Clifford is a fine horsemen and showman. He knows how to wow a crowd from the happy jingling of his conches to his flashy coordinated clothes and thrilling performance."

"He certainly does."

Laura turned to him. Her worry-filled eyes searched his face. "Are you having a change of heart? Do you want to offer Clifford the endorsement contract instead?"

The hint of hurt in Laura's voice made Guy reach for her hand. He placed it in his open palm, then cupped his hand over hers. "Of course not. Papa Fizzy's is an honorable company. We made the offer to Pete Barnes and, unless he turns us down, the contract is his."

His words, meant to reassure, had the opposite effect on Laura. Her hand and arm stiffened.

"You have my word."

A small glimmer of light broke through the worry veiling Laura's eyes. "Thank you."

"What are you doing here? Jack said you were resting due to your leg injury."

"I'm fine." She pulled her hand free of his and gave him a weak smile. "I wanted to see the competition." Laura cleared her throat. "I mean I was curious about the acts auditioning for the open spot in the show."

"I suppose if Jack doesn't hire them on, they are the competition. They move on to another show, right?"

"Yes. That's correct."

Laughter erupted from the group of spectators. Guy looked up. Pete ran after a Shetland pony with a sombrero tied to its head, spinning a lariat through the air. "Pete does other acts for the Western show?"

"Yes, he has several. He's the comedy relief while the hands set up props for the next act." Laura smiled at Guy.

"Doesn't that interfere with preparing for the Buckskin Jones routine?"

Laura's brown eyes widened and a hint of terror settled on her face. She shook her head and turned back to the arena.

Guy frowned at Laura's reaction and watched Pete spin his lasso through the air. It settled gracefully over the pony's hat. "He's quite good with a rope for a lefty."

Casting a sideways glance, Laura shrugged. "He practices a lot."

Pete's antics with the horse made the animal appear to be smarter than the man. Not a concept Guy went for, but maybe it appealed to children. He looked at Laura. "How many routines does Pete perform in a show?"

"Hmm…maybe four." Laura bit her bottom lip and raised her brows at Guy.

"I see." Guy leaned his elbows on his knees, steepled his fingers and rested his chin on them while he continued to watch Pete's comedic performance. Papa Fizzy's wanted to endorse the star of the show, Buckskin Jones; however Pete was easily recognizable during this act, which wasn't quite the image they wanted their soda associated with, was it?

Papa Fizzy's wanted someone with sparkle and pizazz. Someone who caught a consumer's eye. Someone children thought of as heroic. He hated to admit it, but something more like Clifford's act. Perhaps their scouts had pointed them in the wrong direction. He'd need to see the Buckskin Jones act.

"Will he be doing the Buckskin Jones routine this afternoon?"

Laura avoided looking at him. She concentrated on Pete antics. "No." She shook her head. "Pete's just doing this routine because it's new. He's testing it out on an audience."

"I see." Guy rubbed his fingertips over his chin. He'd better call Mr. Turner and run this past him.

"What do you mean by that?" Laura's neck snapped to the side. Fear and fire flickered through her brown eyes—a mix of emotion Guy couldn't read. Why would his simple observation ignite that type of a response?

"I mean, Papa Fizzy's is after an image, a persona, if you will. We thought Buckskin Jones was Pete's exclusive act."

Chapter 9

"We have to tell the truth and sign this contract." The paper rustled under the tremble of Laura's hand. "Now."

The firmness in her voice finally triggered a movement from her father. He lowered the newspaper. His aggravated expression told her he didn't appreciate her commanding tone. Pete flashed a wary-eyed look in her direction. She didn't heed her brother's warning. She stood her ground in front of her father, the coffee table the only barrier between them.

The past eighteen hours had been the longest of her life with her emotions jumping from worry to fear to anger to shame for the secret they were keeping from Guy and the world. He had every right to wonder why their headlining act also performed small comedic acts. Did spectators wonder the same thing during a show? Had Guy seen through their sham?

Add to that Clifford's savvy ability to awe a crowd,

which now included Guy, with his performance. Clifford's hunger for an endorsement contract was so strong, Laura knew he'd stop at nothing to get one.

"I don't want to lose this contract to Clifford." She shook the papers at her father.

"Calm down, Laura." Her father snapped his newspaper to attention before returning it to its original folds. "I spoke with Guy about Pete's involvement in the show and assured him if we signed the contract the only performing Pete would do at our show is the Buckskin Jones act."

A low growl hummed from the back of her throat. Pete didn't perform as Buckskin Jones. "Are you hiring someone to replace Pete for the comedic routines?"

"No, I'm not. We can't afford it. If we sign the contract, Guy will return to the city and Papa Fizzy's will be none the wiser."

"I don't know, Pop. We're already in pretty deep with Laura performing the trick riding and me greeting spectators after the shows. It's a wonder someone hasn't noticed the subtle differences." Pete nervously ran his palms up and down his thigh, swishing the stiff denim of his jeans.

Laura flashed him a smile. It felt good to have someone in her corner. She knew Pete didn't care for the ruse any more than she did. "Clifford might have already picked up on those differences. He's always winking and suggesting he knows who really performs the Buckskin Jones routine."

"Clifford doesn't know anything of the sort. He's just trying to get your feminine attention." Her dad tossed the folded newspaper at the coffee table. It slid across the top and teetered for a second but didn't fall.

Laura exaggerated an eye roll. "Guy needs to see

my act so he knows how much better I am than Clifford." Laura strode into her bedroom, ignoring the burning pain in her calf with every determined step. She grabbed her outfit from behind the clothes in her closet and returned to the living room of their suite.

"He needs to see *me* perform my riding routine wearing this." She teetered a hanger on two fingers, holding her fringed red leather riding skirt with matching vest and white satin blouse for her father to see. "I saw a pair of red cowboy boots at Bell's that I plan to purchase and wear with this outfit when I perform. Me." Laura poked her chest. "*Not* Buckskin Jones. Guy told me his mother wanted to sign a woman trick rider to endorse their cream soda, but someone beat them to Winona. Now they can have me."

A deep frown formed on her father's face. "I am not letting you ride and ruin your reputation. If this skirt slides up while you are in an upside down trick, do you know what men and women will say about you?"

"That isn't going to happen." She tucked the curved end of the wire hanger under her chin and lifted one leg of the riding skirt. "See, I've sewn a bloomer panel with elastic into the leg. Even if the leather flips up, the bloomer will not." She lifted her eyes to watch her father's expression. "Less of my leg will show in this outfit than it does in my everyday dresses."

The frown deepened.

"Guy told us women trick riders draw bigger crowds. Giving me top billing along with this endorsement deal is just what our show needs." Laura let the leather on the leg of her riding skirt drop and removed the hangar from under her chin. She held the outfit closer to her father. "It's almost as flashy as Clifford's outfits. People will love it."

"It is pretty, sis. You did a great job. Don't you think she did a great job, Pop?"

Poor Pete. Always in the middle and always trying to give Laura credit for her abilities.

"Laura's talents aren't in question. She is a fine seamstress and excellent trick rider. Her reputation is what's on the line. It's bad enough having Clifford and Guy act like buck deer ready to clash antlers over her. I'm not having every cowboy in the county acting that way, thinking she's the same caliber woman Winona Phelps is—a tart."

Her father stood, casting a shadow over Laura.

"You know I'd never act that way. I have no desire to see the inside of a billiard room or experience the taste of tobacco or whiskey. You raised me in a good Christian home. I know the type of behavior you and God expect of me. I won't let either of you down. Can't you let me try to use my talent under my own name?" The tension in the room grew heavier than the hanger dangling from two fingers on her left hand.

"I am letting you try. I agreed to let you go on an afternoon date with Guy. He has fine manners and treats you with respect."

Laura wanted to growl. Did her dad really think he was doing her a favor by allowing her to go on a date with Guy? Her only interest in Guy was finding out information.

"Speaking of which." Checking his watch, her dad glared at Laura. "Enough of this conversation. He's liable to hear through the door. You will continue to ride as Buckskin Jones and that's final." He poked the air with his index finger.

Out of the corner of her eye, Laura saw Pete slide down in his chair a few inches. His stance admitted defeat and spoke louder than words. Laura couldn't count on him to jump into this argument. Laura narrowed her eyes and stuck out her index finger, mirroring her dad's posture. "Someday you'll be sorry for this." She turned on her heel, intending to march into her bedroom, when a gentle knock sounded on the door.

Laura hugged her outfit and ran on her tiptoes to her room, kicking the door closed with her shoe heel. She placed the hanger over a hook on the back of her bedroom door and drew a deep breath to steady her nerves.

After the confrontation with her father, the last person she wanted to see was Guy. His opinions too closely matched her father's. Laura frowned. Many of Guy's qualities reminded her of her father. She walked over to the bureau mirror and smoothed a hand down her hair. Would she see the appreciative glow shining in his cobalt eyes this afternoon? She sighed

The men's muted voices carried through the bedroom door. She tapped the apples of her cheeks with her fingertips, enhancing the natural pink of her skin. Apprehension circled through her like a spinning lasso through the air. How could she want to see Guy and *not* want to see Guy at the same time? It made no sense.

Maybe it was the excitement of finally getting the answers to her questions. Her body trembled with nervous energy. No, this was a date, not a business meeting. If Guy refused to talk shop, then what would they talk about? The thought hadn't occurred to her before. Laura bit her lower lip.

"Laura, Guy's here." Her dad's voice boomed through the closed door.

Standing in front of the mirror, she gave herself one last assessment. She chose to wear nylons under her sailor outfit. She twisted her leg. The navy pleated skirt's hemline hid most of the bruise, so the sliver of blue–purple skin, in the shape of a fingernail moon, wasn't too obvious.

Laura gave a quick glance at her closet, wishing she'd made something new to wear. *What are you doing?* It didn't matter if Guy had seen this outfit. Did it?

She jumped when the door rattled under the hard rap of her father's knuckles. "Laura."

"I'm coming." She slipped her straw cloche over her head and adjusted the hat band, made of wide, navy ribbon with red piping sewed down the middle so the bow sat a little off center. She picked up her handbag, drew a deep breath and opened the bedroom door.

Guy stood behind the table of ledgers, pointing out something to her father. Laura's lips twitched into a smile. He'd chosen the double-breasted suit jacket and Oxford bags he'd worn the day he arrived in Cottonwood Landing. Somehow seeing him in familiar clothing made her feel better about her repeat outfit.

When Guy looked up, he smiled. "Laura, you are looking lovely, as always."

Laura's smile widened despite Pete's muffled snort at Guy's compliment. "I'm sorry I kept you waiting."

"That's quite all right. I wanted to show Jack a figure I questioned. It's a carryover balance." For a brief second, Guy looked at her father. "Could I review the previous year's ledger?"

"I suppose."

Guy's eyes found Laura's line of vision. She wasn't even certain he heard her father's reply. He stepped around the table and walked toward her. "Shall we?"

Laura slipped her hand in the crook of his arm and allowed him to guide her to the door. After he opened it, Laura stepped through. Guy started to close the door behind them, then stopped. "Sir, I plan to deliver Laura back to the suite after an early supper."

He closed the door before her father could protest or question him further. A thrill shot through Laura at Guy's boldness. He told her father what he planned to do. He didn't ask permission.

"The heat and humidity are unrelenting today. I thought we could enjoy a treat at the soda fountain, then relax in the park before having a light supper at the diner, if you find that acceptable."

Both perfect venues for conversation. "It sounds lovely. There is nothing else I'd rather do."

The small soda fountain in the back of the drug store had eight stools attached to the marble-topped counter and three small tables with wire-backed chairs.

"I'd prefer a table." Laura didn't know the young man working behind the counter, but she didn't want anyone to hear their conversation. "Is that one okay?" She pointed to the table close to the wall sitting the farthest away from the young man.

Guy nodded and followed her to the table, holding her chair while she slipped onto the hard wooden seat.

"What may I order for you?"

"Sit down, he'll come over in a minute and I'll tell him then." Laura waved her hand at the chair across the table.

When Guy didn't sit, she looked up at him. His lips were pursed. Not in an angry way, more of a perplexed way. "Laura, in polite settings, gentlemen order for ladies."

Laura puckered her lips. None of the men she knew ordered for their wives, but she liked the idea of falling under the "lady" category.

"You may order anything you like."

"Okay. A root-beer float sounds scrumptious."

Guy nodded, walked over to the counter and placed their order. When he returned he pulled the empty chair at the table closer to Laura.

"What did you order?" Guy's nearness made Laura feel awkward. Her hands seemed large and grew heavy. She didn't know what to do with them. Finally she rested them on top of her purse, which was lying in her lap.

"A strawberry malted with two straws and two spoons in the event we want to sample one another's treat."

The sheepish look on Guy's face and her trembling nerves drew out a high-pitched giggle. Laura tried to stop it. She failed, and for a few seconds she sounded like the teenage girls that gathered around Pete after a Buckskin Jones performance.

Laura tensed under her frustration at her response. What was it about Guy that made her giddy?

Guy leaned back in his chair while Laura racked her brain for something to say to lead into a discussion about business. She took a deep breath. "I know it's not as exciting as a big city, but are you enjoying your time here in Cottonwood Landing?"

Removing his homburg, Guy placed it on the table. "Going over the Western show's book work is quite exhilarating. Your income and expense basis is very different from Papa Fizzy's, which makes it a challenge and quite interesting."

His beautiful eyes looked at her, but Laura was certain he was seeing ledger lines and penciled figures in his mind.

"I'm glad." Laura knew lining up numbers in a neat

and orderly fashion still added up to their show needing the endorsement contract.

Guy's genuine smile calmed some of her nerves. "I know not everyone gets excited about accounting work. But I do. It's an essential part of business and I want to head the department at Papa Fizzy's." The high tin-paneled ceiling caught Guy's sigh and echoed it back. "Your father has trusted me with all of his ledgers. The only accounting papers at Papa Fizzy's I've been allowed to review are the income and expense reports."

Laura's heart turned to soft leather and bent at the wistful look that washed over Guy's face. He wanted to work in the accounting department at Papa Fizzy's as much as she wanted to drop the character act and ride under her own name, maybe more.

The scuff of the counter boy's heels on the plank floor stopped Laura from speaking. She leaned back to allow him to place her root-beer float on the table. "Thank you." She smiled politely at the young man.

She pushed the wax-paper straw to the bottom of the glass and took a sip of the tangy root beer. The cool liquid laced with melting ice cream refreshed her. She lifted a spoonful of the vanilla ice cream from the top of the glass. "It's your dream to work in the accounting department, isn't it?"

Taking her bite of ice cream, she watched Guy's features light up.

"Yes, it is. How could you tell?" Guy pumped his straw through the thick, pink malted.

"Happiness shines from your face when you talk about it." Laura sipped from her straw.

"I wish Mother could see it." Guy sighed. "My mother held our family together after my grandfather's accident and my father died. She made sure I went to the best boarding schools, even when I'd rather have stayed close to home and attended the public school right down the street. I know she must have been lonely with me gone, but she continued to do her charity work while running the household and caring for Grandfather. She's managed to grant me my every wish, except for my career."

Laura stopped eating and rested her chin in her hand. Guy's life held familiar similarities to hers. He'd lost a parent when he was young. He had dreams he was unable to chase. Something shifted in her heart. They were kindred spirits. "I understand completely. My father is the same way. I've asked, pleaded and, I'm ashamed to say, begged, yet, he won't allow me to follow my dream."

Until Guy clasped her hand and squeezed, Laura hadn't realized she'd reached out for him. She'd been so drawn by the fact someone else might sympathize with her feelings, she didn't even realize what she'd just said. She'd said something about her dream.

Their unfulfilled dreams. Guy had finally seemed to break through the barrier between him and Laura. "What stops you from following your dream? Your father needing you at the show?"

For a moment, Laura drew her brows together, wrinkling her forehead and nose. A perplexed look crossed her face. "Yes, that's it. I stay because he needs my help with the show, and I'm trying to follow God's commandment and honor my father."

Happiness swelled Guy's chest. Laura had another trait he wanted in a wife. She was a grounded Christian. "God's commandments are the best rules to follow." He squeezed her delicate hand, savoring the softness of her skin. "I'm here for the same reason. I'm trying to follow God's rule and honor my mother."

Laura wiggled her fingers, interlocking them with Guy's. "You are a fine example of a Christian. Your kindness shows in your actions and your smile. You were so concerned for my well-being the other day and, well, I don't think I thanked you properly. So, thank you, Guy Roberts, for your concern."

Intense emotion swirled through Guy. He wanted to lean forward and brush his lips against hers, which wasn't proper in a public place. The last thing he'd want to do is tarnish Laura's reputation. He lifted their hands. With a slight twist to his wrist, he brought her hand to his lips. He pressed a kiss into the silky skin just below her knuckles. He breathed in her faint honeysuckle aroma before lowering their joined hands to the table.

Tenderness veiled Laura's brown eyes. She'd placed her free hand on her chest. She'd seemed surprised by his show of emotion. Was she also delighted? He was and couldn't tell if the feeling was shared.

"I'm sorry. I shouldn't have been so cavalier. Please forgive me." Guy pulled his fingers free.

"No, I won't forgive you and I don't want you to be sorry." Laura blinked several times.

"I don't want to be making unwanted advances."

"You aren't." Laura's eyes widened at the loudness of her voice and she looked around the drugstore. Laura returned her gaze to Guy. She opened her lips, then closed them, her hesitation evident. In seconds her face registered resolve. "I like you very much." She'd lowered her voice to barely a whisper.

She shared his feelings. This business trip was turning out to be a pleasure.

Chapter 10

"Let me help you with your package." Guy stood, rounded the table and quickly walked over to Laura. A smile had been plastered to his face since their date two days ago, and now it widened. He'd missed Laura at the hotel every time he'd come to call no matter the hour.

He lifted the large rectangular box from her arms. "You've been to Bell's."

"Yes, I have." Laura pulled lace gloves from her hands. She turned to close the suite's door. She could hear the maid humming in the other room. "The humming doesn't bother you?"

"No, quite the opposite. She's been singing hymns while she works, which I find soothing. Where can I put this for you?"

"Follow me." Laura slipped off her unadorned cloche and strode toward the door of her room. She opened the width to a narrow crack and stood aside. "Please sit it on top of the bureau."

The bureau was only two steps into the room. Guy nodded, slipping through the crack of the door and keeping his eyes focused on his destination. Once the parcel was secure on the furniture top, he turned.

A hanger, still swinging from the movement of the door being opened, clicked against the door. Red fringed leather riding pants caught his eye. Although it wasn't proper he stopped to look at the outfit hanging on the back of the door.

He reached out and pinched the soft red leather between his thumb and forefinger. His eyes roamed the hanger. It was the type of outfit he thought he'd see all of the women who worked around the Western show wearing.

He lifted the hanger from the door and stepped into the living quarters of the suite. "Did you make this?"

"Oh." Laura breathed fear into the word. "You weren't supposed to see my outfit."

"Why? It's beautiful." Guy laid the outfit over the back of the davenport and inspected the seam construction. "French. You are a very talented seamstress."

Laura walked across the room. "You think so?"

"Yes, I do. Is this your own design?"

"Not really. I used a pattern but altered it." Excitement toned Laura's voice. "I sewed bloomer panels into the legs to allow for movement on a horse while still keeping propriety by not showing an inappropriate amount of leg."

A fetching blush colored Laura's face and matched the deep pink of the plaid dress she wore. "You are very talented." *And beautiful.* His heart added its opinion.

His feelings for Laura were strong. "Are these the types of costumes you sew for the Western show?"

"Most aren't quite this special. Pete and Dad don't go for flashy costumes like Clifford wears. I construct jackets from corduroy or matching Western shirts for them. Of course, some of Pete's comedic acts require adornments on his costumes, patches on the britches…"

Laura's descriptions stopped abruptly. Guy realized he'd frowned at her last description. He'd try to call Mr. Tuner to see if his business consensus was the same. Pete Barnes must perform exclusively as Buckskin Jones or there was no endorsement deal. Of course, Mr. Turner wasn't in his office, so Guy called and spoke with his mother. She supported Guy's reaction to the comedic acts.

"Please continue."

Laura shook her head. "I should put this away." She lifted the hanger.

"Do you wear this costume during the show?"

The dim sunlight streaming through the heavy curtains cast shadows through the room, making it hard to see. Guy thought Laura's eyes misted over. She pursed her lips and shook her head. "No. I don't wear this in the show. No one does."

Laura hugged the hanger to her chest. It must be the part of her dream her father didn't support. Although tears never sprang to his eyes when his mother's ideas for his future didn't agree with his own, disappointment wrung his heart until he thought it might twist right out of his chest. He hated that Laura felt the same pain. She'd probably designed this dress in hopes of going to school or starting a dress-making business.

Guy had many business connections in Sioux City. His mother had more social connections. Together they'd be able to secure a seamstress position for Laura. The next time he spoke with his mother, he'd mention it. In a few days, he hoped to take a signed endorsement contract and Laura back to the city with him—that is if Jack could spare Pete for a few days to accompany them until Laura was settled into a room in his mother's home. Then Guy would pay for Pete's train ticket back to the show.

He watched Laura cross the room, open the door and return the outfit to its place on the hook. He imagined the happiness on her face when he told her he could help fulfill her dream. For now, he'd keep his plan a secret until all of the pieces could fall into place. Of course, she'd only be an enterprising young lady until he had a chance to court her and win her heart. After their marriage, his mother could teach her the finer points of running a household and the advantages of selecting the right social contacts to help Papa Fizzy's grow and succeed.

"Would you care for a cup of coffee?" Laura walked to a round table tucked in a corner of the room. A copper tea kettle sat on a small hot plate. Beside it was an aluminum drip coffeepot. Laura tipped up the lid of the kettle before bending to plug in the hot plate.

"Yes, thank you." Guy glanced at the table filled with ledgers. Jack had produced the two previous years' books for him to review. Although the puzzle of the discrepancy he found called to his logical mind, for once in his life he allowed his heart to rule the situation. He took a seat on the davenport.

The scrape of the coffee canister's tin lid squeaked through the room. The familiar tinkling of the measuring spoon tapping against the coffee's container and the reassembling of the water reservoir to the pot reminded

Guy of the comforts of home. He watched Laura efficiently ready the pot for water and place cups on saucers. His mind's eye placed Laura in a large roomy kitchen, preparing breakfast for him before he journeyed downtown to the business office of the soda company. Who'd have dreamed he'd find his future wife at a Wild West show?

"You take two sugars, right?"

His body started when Laura's voice woke him from his pleasant daydream. "I'm sorry?"

"You put two spoonfuls of sugar in your coffee, right?" Laura held a heaping spoon of granules over one of the mugs.

"Yes, I do."

"I prefer to put it in the bottom of the cup, then pour the coffee on top. I think it dissolves better." She finished putting sugar in both mugs, lifted the tea kettle and poured the hot liquid into the pot's reservoir. After she placed the lid on the pot, she unplugged the hot-plate cord.

In a few minutes she'd join him on the davenport and they could get to know each other better.

"Did you find out the answer to my question from the other day?" Laura stood patiently waiting for the water to drip through the coffeepot.

She'd asked him many business questions on the afternoon they'd spent in the park. "Which one?"

"Are there really shifty managers who exploit their clients and steal their money?"

Guy fought a frown. He'd found the question odd. "No, I've found no facts to support that scenario. However, I've met some less than honorable business people, so I'm sure there's some truth to the rumor."

The pucker of her lips and sag of her shoulders indicated his answer wasn't what Laura had hoped to hear.

"Is your father thinking of hiring a business manager?" In Guy's opinion, what Jack needed to hire was an accountant. Even the rudimentary set of books Jack Barnes kept weren't accurate. If he continued this way, it'd only be a matter of time before their business folded. After Guy put the books in order, he planned to suggest that Jack have someone else keep his ledgers.

"Oh, no. Dad doesn't have a high opinion of business managers." Laura lifted the pot and poured the steaming dark liquid into the cups.

Jack's voice boomed down the hall as he greeted the maid. He and Pete stepped into the room and squinted until their eyes adjusted to the dim light of the room.

"Good afternoon, Mr. Barnes, Pete." Guy stood, holding out his hand to greet the men.

"Guy. I've told you to call me Jack." He emphasized his request with a firm handshake. Pete's weak grip brought a reminder to Guy of another thing to discuss with his mother—how to address this problem before Pete greeted the public on behalf of Papa Fizzy's.

Laura set the saucers with the filled cups on the coffee table. "Would either of you care for coffee?"

"None for me, sis." Pete slipped onto the end of the davenport to Guy's left.

"Yes, I'll have a cup." Jack smiled at his daughter and sunk into the open corner of the davenport. Guy's heart dipped. He'd planned to have Laura sit next to him.

"I'm glad we're all here." Jack took the proffered saucer from Laura.

She picked up her cup and settled into the wingback chair in the intimate gathering of furniture.

"I've been thinking, Guy. Laura made a valid point about having Starlight added to the contract."

Laura's cup rattled against the saucer. Using two hands, she placed it on the table. She scooted to the edge of her chair, her eyes fixed on her father. Happiness settled on her face, enhancing her beauty.

"Pete and I discussed it. We feel the contract should include all aspects of the Buckskin Jones character, which includes Starlight."

Guy straightened his shoulders, ready to tell Jack the addition wasn't acceptable. They weren't adding a dangerous beast to the endorsement contract.

"Oh, Dad."

Laura's breathy words drew a stern stare from her father. An urge to defend Laura surged through Guy. Although he agreed with Jack that business was no place for a woman, he did feel Jack was too strict with Laura. Jack had raised a perfect lady in the midst of wild beasts and a gypsy band of showmen. If Laura was his wife he'd never treat her with such disrespect.

To Guy's surprise, Laura didn't display the same reaction to her father's stare. A wide, satisfied smile increased the happiness on her face tenfold.

The strong emotions Laura invoked in Guy shoved his disgruntled feeling toward Jack aside. Laura's bliss magnified her loveliness. How could he disappoint her? He swallowed his denial of the request, not wanting to be the person to erase this happy moment for Laura.

"Well, I'll have to contact Mr. Turner and my mother about this issue. I want you all to know—" Guy looked at Jack and then Pete before settling his gaze on Laura

"—this has potential to be a huge liability to the company and the answer may be no."

Since Guy reviewed the books, he felt certain Papa Fizzy's could counter-negotiate this addition to the contract by offering more money and never adding the horse.

"We'll cross the bridge when we get there." Jack drew a long drink from his coffee.

"You still haven't met Starlight." Laura clapped her hands together. "I think once you see what a gentle horse she is you'll change your mind about her being a liability."

"Laura makes a valid point. You need to come out to the fairgrounds and meet Starlight." Jack finished his coffee and set the cup and saucer on the coffee table.

Like a chance acquaintance with an old friend, fear wrapped Guy in a tight hug, reminding him of his past experiences with horses. His hand started to tremble, rattling the china cup against the saucer.

Using both hands, he placed his coffee on the table in front of him. He drew a deep breath. It was useless in settling his nerves. He'd admired Clifford's abilities with his horses a few days ago from a distance. The thought of being close enough for a horse to rear up and bring their deadly legs down on top of him beaded sweat on his lip and palpitated his heart.

"Yes, one of these days I need to visit the other star of the show." He forced a smile in Pete's direction, hoping no one saw through his brave façade. He stood and pulled his watch from his jeans pocket. He checked the time. "If you'll excuse me, I'll try to contact Mr. Turner or my mother concerning this matter."

Stepping over Pete's outstretched frame, Guy crossed

the room on trembling legs, praying he'd make it to the door before fear buckled his knees.

It'd been two days since her father had spoken with Guy, trying to negotiate the addition of Starlight. Laura smiled and pulled the halter decorated with leather stars over Starlight's muzzle.

"You're a good girl." Laura petted her paint's nose while she slipped the bit in her mouth.

Laura had been walking on cloud nine. Her father had used her suggestion. She felt one step closer to convincing her dad to let her perform under her own name.

Doubled-checking the bridle, halter and saddle, Laura ensured they were securely in place. She patted her horse's rump. "Starlight, this might feel a little different today. It does to me."

She looked down. In the dim light of the moon she admired her new red boots sticking out from under her red leather riding skirt. The dew-dampened morning air soaked through the satin of her blouse, chilling her skin. In a few moments, her vigorous routine would chase away the gooseflesh.

Taking a running start, Laura grabbed the saddle horn, gave a small jump and pulled herself into the saddle. Under her legs' commands, Starlight galloped around the arena. The billowing sleeves of her blouse snapped in the wind. With practiced accuracy, Laura turned backward in her saddle. She maneuvered her leg over the high saddle horn and slipped her left foot into the right stirrup. Once her footing was in place, she held on to the saddle horn with her left hand and lifted her right hand into the air while straightening her right leg parallel to Starlight's body.

Starlight took two laps around the arena while Laura

held the side layout stance. The stiffness of the new leather of her boots added a few seconds of time to her dismount of the side layout. She'd need to break them in more. Laura repeated each trick in her routine twice to learn her footing in her new boots. Tangerine hues colored the horizon. She knew she was running out of darkness, but she only had the finale left.

Positioning her feet in the stirrups Laura adjusted the reins, let go and fell backward over Starlight's rump. Her hands dangled by Starlight's tail. She watched the bleachers and fencing go by in a blur. She gauged a six-second interval and was ready to raise her body up when a blur of white caught her eyes. Frowning, she lifted her body and regained her balance.

By the time she stood in the hippodrome, her ending stance, Starlight had circled back to the arena area where she had seen the flash of white. Right side up and standing high in the saddle, she saw the white form. Clifford's horses.

The faint jingle of their conches rang in the sunrise behind them. Only a few feet from the arena, Clifford reined his horses to a stop and waved to Laura. As she swallowed hard, her fingers made contact with her reins and she slid back into the saddle.

How long had Clifford been in the area? How much of her routine did he see? Her eyesight blurred the horses, making them appear to be in the distance. They might not have been very far away. It was hard to gauge anything hanging upside down over the backside of a horse.

If Clifford only witnessed her riding around the arena doing the hippodrome trick, it wasn't a problem. The only trick she couldn't let people see her do was the back drag. She prayed dawn's shadows and the fencing prohibited Clifford from seeing her doing Buckskin Jones's special feat.

Her heart dropped to her stomach. He stood on his horses to ride. She knew how far a person could see sixteen hands high. She lifted her hand in the air and reined Starlight to a stop beside the fence.

"'Morning." Clifford flashed her a knowing smile.

"Good morning."

"I came out to exercise my horses. I'm waiting for a yay or nay from Jack on whether he wants to contract me for one of the acts. If it's a nay I'm planning on heading over to Colonel Cooper's show."

"Oh." Nerves and worry prohibited her from saying anything else.

"Now you know why I'm here." Clifford pushed his hat back. Ringlets fell over his forehead. A cocky smile curled his lips. He crossed his arms over his chest. "Mind telling me what you're doing here at this early hour dressed in such a fancy getup?"

Chapter 11

"Just exercising Starlight." Laura gave the horse loose rein, allowing the paint to turn in small circles.

"Didn't I see you doing a trick?" Clifford's smirk curled deep and wide, wrinkling the skin around his eyes.

Laura's heart took off at a trot, forcing the air out of her lungs in rapid pants. Her eyes roamed the horizon behind him. She tried to gauge the distance he'd been from the fence when she'd noticed the white blur. Had he seen her in the back drag? She racked her brain on how to answer his question and decided to give him more rope. Let him tell her what he saw. She nodded her head.

"Can you do other tricks besides the hippodrome?"

Again, she nodded. "A few easy ones." The answer wasn't a lie and still honored her father's wishes, yet humiliation tore through her. She wanted so badly to show the world her talent and get credit for her abilities.

"Too bad you can't perform in your father's show. Guess he doesn't need two trick riders, though." Clifford's eyes narrowed. "Maybe you should try auditioning for Colonel Cooper." He snapped his fingers. "No, he has Winona Phelps, the *best* girl trick rider on the circuit. Guess he wouldn't need two trick riders, either." Clifford punctuated his statements with an exaggerated finger snap.

Was he trying to goad the truth out of her? Sadly, if he was, it was working. She wanted to spit out a rebuttal to his last statement. Instead, Laura pursed her lips to keep from biting out the things she wanted to say to Clifford.

"Laura." She twisted in the saddle. Pete leaned out the driver's window on their old pickup. "You need to get to the hotel, clean up and eat breakfast. We have a contract meeting with Guy at nine."

"Okay, meet me in the stable." Laura knew Pete would help her brush down Starlight and muck her stall.

Laura flashed Clifford a smug smile. Turnabout was fair play after all. "This is an important meeting. We're ready to sign the endorsement contract. I'd better get going. The arena's all yours." Waving Clifford off with the wiggle of her fingers, Laura clicked her tongue and Starlight galloped off with her rider's worries trailing close behind.

Guy paced behind the table housing the Wild West show's books. It seemed everything and everyone had turned against him. His mother delighted in the idea of adding Starlight to the contract. His eardrum still throbbed from the squeal that came through the phone line.

He'd left a message for Mr. Turner, hoping he'd see the senselessness and liability of adding a horse to the endorsement contract. His mother returned the call, saying Mr. Turner was away on business. He'd so wanted to tell his mother to fire Mr. Turner and appoint him to the chief accountant post.

His aggravation stoked the furnace of his anger until he thought smoke might puff out of his ears. How could he make his mother understand an executive needed to be in the office to run a profitable business? Guy sighed, releasing some of his pent-up steam in his exhale. It was a futile fight. His mother knew nothing about business and trusted the board's opinion on the staffing at Papa Fizzy's.

Letting his gaze drop to the thick ledgers, Guy shook his head. Even his constant comfort, numbers, weren't adding up today. Something was wrong with Jack's ledgers. He'd gone back a year and three quarters and still couldn't find the discrepancy. Yet anyone could see the debits added up to more than credits on every page. His balance should be red, not black.

Guy scratched his head. Although it was a lot of work, he'd have to recreate Jack's ledger with receipts. He stuck his hand in the overflowing shoe box and rustled the papers with his thumb.

Pulling his watch from his jeans pocket, he checked the time. The Barnes family should be finished with breakfast and on their way back to the suite. He drew a deep breath. The terms of the endorsement weren't to his liking. He'd practiced saying "We'll add Starlight to the contract" until he'd found a happy medium between excited and matter of fact. At least he'd removed the trembling from his voice.

This new twist to the contract would please Laura. The nervous energy coursing through Guy changed to excitement at the thought of Laura's bliss. It filled him with joy to see her jubilation. He wanted to make her happy not just today but every day for the rest of their lives. Many times when she looked at him a tender expression crossed her eyes. He suspected her feelings were stronger than just enjoying his company.

Shaking his head, Guy smiled. The change to the contract meant yet again extending his stay in Cottonwood Landing while the new contract was drawn up. It'd take a few days to revise the legal document and a few more for the general delivery letter to reach the hotel.

His mother apologized when she told him Mr. Turner felt he needed to stay put. However, no apology was necessary. His heart jumped at the chance to spend more time in Laura's company, even though danger lurked around every corner at the fairgrounds. So far, he'd managed to avoid coming face to face with one of the dangerous beasts. This ledger mess assured his continued safety.

The twist of the bolt releasing drew Guy from his thoughts. Laura burst through the door. Her rosy cheeks accentuated the dark brown of her eyes. She wore a yellow skirt with an off-white middy blouse. Always in vogue, she'd fit in easily in the city, and her slender form was a perfect showcase for her sewing abilities. A job Guy didn't plan for her to hold long.

Jack and Pete followed her through the door in their normal work attire, denim jeans and faded plaid shirts.

"Why don't we all sit down?" Guy motioned to the small round table in the corner.

The Barnes men flanked Laura's sides, leaving Guy to sit directly across from her. The hope on her face added to her loveliness.

"Mr. Turner was out of the office so I spoke with my mother. She believes in the benefit of adding Starlight." Guy paused to allow the tremor of fear at the back of his throat to subside.

Laura lean forward, her eyes wide with expectancy.

Clearing his throat, Guy spoke rapidly in an effort to beat the fear threatening to shake his voice. "She believes the benefit of adding Buckskin Jones's horse outweighs any possible liabilities."

"Really?" Laura jumped up from her seat. The momentum tipped the straight-backed chair and it clamored to the floor. She rapidly clapped her hands before resting her praying hands against her lips.

Guy didn't quite understand this much exuberance in altering the contract.

"Laura, sit down." Jack shook his head at his daughter's excitement while trying to hide a smile.

Pete stood and righted the chair. "Does the money increase?"

Laura stopped her one-woman celebration and looked at her brother dumbfounded before she turned to Guy. "Is there more money?"

"No. Papa Fizzy's does not pay animals to endorse their product. The monetary figure remains the same. We are only adding Starlight to photo shoots and some personal appearances."

Guy inflected firmness in his tone.

"That's okay. I just wondered." Pete shrugged.

"Then the contract meets your approval and you'll sign on to endorse our product?"

Before he answered, Pete did a peculiar thing. He looked to his father, then to Laura, who gave a slight nod. Pete turned to Guy. "Yes, it does. If you give me the contract I'll read the changes, sign it and return it to you tomorrow."

"Because we altered the contract, we'll have to wait for a new one to arrive. I expect it here by the end of the week. I hope you find that agreeable."

All of the Barnes family nodded their heads. Guy found it agreeable, too. He had two things to do while he waited. Whip the show books into shape and convince Laura to return to Sioux City with him.

Laura stepped across the threshold and skidded to a stop on the worn area rug in front of their suite's door. Buckskin clad, she hadn't expected Guy to be up early working on the books. Thankfully, the floor lamp he'd pulled to the corner of the table illuminated his work area so his presence didn't startle her.

His piercing gaze and pursed lips showed his displeasure at her attire. "You're too lovely a young lady to be dressed in a manly fashion."

Laura's heart teetered between hurt and elation. His disapproving expression hurt her and induced shame for being a part of the Buckskin Jones sham. She agreed wholeheartedly with him. She shouldn't be dressed this way. She should be practicing in a cowgirl outfit similar to her show costume. Had he just called her lovely? Yes, he had. Her heart's scales tipped to the elation side.

A giddy thrill spun through her, threatening to come out in a squeal.

With effort, Laura forced nonchalance into her voice

and closed the door. "Why are you here so early?" Guy seldom started on their bookwork before nine o'clock. By Laura's calculations, it could barely be past seven. She squinted to see the hands of the clock in the shadowed room.

Rubbing his eyes, Guy spread a hand out over the book work. "I'm perplexed by these figures. I can't tell if this is a five or a two." Guy sighed. "I never struggle with numbers."

"Perhaps you need a break?" Laura walked over to the table and lifted the slip of paper he dropped in exasperation. "This is Dad's handwriting. It's a five. See the small mark here?" She drew her finger over the line. "His twos resemble a question mark."

"How about this one?" Guy lifted another receipt from the pile.

"That's Pete's handwriting." She squinted her eyes and lifted the paper to the brightness of the light bulb. "That's a one. It's hard to tell his ones from sevens, but see the small pencil line there?" Again, she used her finger to underline. "It's a one."

"Why, that's barely a mark!" Guy held the paper close.

"I know." Laura shrugged. "If you need to verify anything else, let me know. I'm going to change now."

Guy's eye's widened. A flush crawled up his neck. "I met your father and brother in the hallway. They assured me the suite was empty. I never imagined…" Guy rose and strode across the floor. "I can continue my pursuit of numbers later. If you'll excuse me." He reached for the doorknob.

Laura's heart pattered at Guy's concern for her reputation. "I'll only be a few minutes. Then I plan to make a pot of coffee. Would you care to join me for a cup?"

"I'd be pleased to. I've been meaning to talk to you about your career. If I drive to the bakery and pick up cinnamon rolls to go with our coffee, will that give you enough time to change?"

It took every ounce of her control to not alter her expression. What did he mean by career? She nodded her head and tried to return his happy smile.

Once he closed the door, Laura slumped against the wall. Did he know? She looked down at her practice buckskins. She was becoming too careless. First with Clifford and now Guy. She might not want to pretend to be someone else as she performed death-defying tricks, but it's what her father wanted and she needed to honor him and adhere to God's instructions.

She prepared the coffee and then paced in a circle around the davenport as the patter of the liquid dripping into the aluminum pot megaphoned through their suite. Did Guy *and* Clifford know that she was Buckskin Jones?

She stopped her nervous walking and rubbed her temple. Guy couldn't possibly know. He'd only been to the fairgrounds twice. Clifford had acted like he knew even before he caught her practicing the routine.

Laura sighed and looked at the clock. Guy should be back any minute. She sponged off Starlight's odor, patted on honeysuckle-scented talcum powder and slipped on her pink broadcloth dress in record time.

Nerves propelled her into motion again. Halfway around the davenport a soft rapping sounded at the door.

"Guy?" Laura hurried over and opened the door. Her heart somersaulted at his wide smile. The twinkle in his cobalt eyes mesmerized her, making it difficult to look away. She knew this was part of what her father feared. Why he didn't want her to be the star of the show. She'd be exposed to strangers with this same look of appreciation in their eyes, strangers who might try to lead her astray. Heat crawled up her neck and burst onto her cheeks. Her heart danced under Guy's gaze like a nervous horse skittered in a stall. Still, she couldn't look away. Didn't want to look away.

"Laura, you look lovely." Guy stepped through the door, strode to the table and began to remove the rolls from the waxed paper bag. "I saw your father and Pete in the lobby. Jack said he'll be up in a few minutes to answer some of my questions concerning the book work."

Closing the door, Laura walked to the table on shaky legs from the bubbly feeling caused by Guy's compliment. Then she remembered this was a conversation she shouldn't be having. What would she tell him if he asked her if she was Buckskin Jones?

Dread pressed down on her and popped her bubbles of happiness. She didn't want to lie to Guy. She liked the fact he held her in high esteem. If she told him the truth, she'd watch the glimmer of appreciation turn to disgust; he'd made his feelings on women trick riders perfectly clear.

Agitation looped through her. She began to tap her toe. "What is it you want to speak to me about?" She managed to keep her tone conversational.

Guy turned, caught her hands in his and gave them a squeeze. "I want to help you make your dreams come true."

Although Guy's expression shined with joy, panic thumped through Laura. He must know about the family secret. Had something in the book work given it away? She tried to turn her expression to stone. If he knew, would he really be willing to help her achieve her dream? Keeping any sign of wariness from her voice, she simply asked, "What?"

"Oh, please sit down." Guy released her hands. "I'll pour the coffee." He removed two cups and saucers from a corner shelf above the table. "I'm afraid I got a little carried away. That is so unlike me."

Yes, it is. Other than the first day they met, Guy had always been logical and in complete control of his emotions. Laura sat down on a straight-backed chair.

"I've been thinking about the conversation we had on our date about our unrealized dreams." Guy pulled his chair close to Laura. "I think I can help you reach your goal."

"You can?" This time her skepticism resounded through the room.

"May I ask you a rather personal question?"

Laura nodded at Guy's earnest expression.

"Do you make all the clothing for you and your family?"

"Yes." Laura continued to nod.

"I thought so. You are a fine seamstress. The Western outfit you showed me the other day is outstanding. It'd be very fitting for someone, say Winona Phelps, to wear in the arena for her show."

"What?" Laura's question exploded from her and ended on a high note that bounced around the room like her father's megaphoned voice echoed through the air when he talked to the crowds.

"I can see you're surprised I figured out your dream. Laura, I hope you'll return to the city with me. With my mother's social contacts and my business associates in Sioux City, I'm certain we can help you get a seamstress position in one of the finer ladies' stores downtown."

"Seam…" Laura stopped. Guy didn't know the secret. He thought she wanted to design or sew clothing. He had no idea that she was Buckskin Jones.

"Yes, seamstress. You have experience making costumes for your father's show. Although…" Guy looked past her shoulders and fixed his gaze on the corner where the table filled with ledgers sat. "I do believe he overpays you for your sewing contributions to the show."

That's because I'm not only a seamstress, but the star of the show. Laura's eyes widened at her thought. Guy began to drag his gaze from the corner. She couldn't look at him or chance voicing her thoughts.

She grabbed a cup. The quick movement splashed coffee over the china's lip and onto the saucer. Laura leaned toward the table and began gulping the bitter liquid, trying to wash her words from the tip of her tongue.

Poor Guy. He had no idea. His intentions were sincere. He'd added two and two together, her position with the show and the Western outfit, and come up with the most logical explanation—that she dreamed of becoming a seamstress or dress designer.

Her heart sank at his expectant look. She glanced away and fitted the bottom of the cup in the small circle of the saucer. She'd never be confined to a sewing machine all day. It was a fun hobby, but nothing could match the freedom she felt on the back of Starlight.

What could she do or say to Guy to squelch this silly notion? She wanted to choose her words carefully. She needed to keep the Buckskin Jones secret, yet spare Guy from hurt feelings because he'd misunderstood.

She drew a deep breath and forced a smile. "That is a very generous offer. However, I don't think it's something my father would allow."

"I've already considered that aspect. I plan to have

my mother speak to him. She'll assure him that she runs a very Christian household, and you'd only associate with the most respectable people."

Laura smiled. "There is no doubt in my mind your mother runs a Christian household. Your actions are a testament to your mother's teaching."

"Thank you." Guy's smile faded. "It doesn't always seem like she sees it that way, though." The brightness in his eyes dulled and disappointment tinged his voice. "She's a wonderful mother and I try to honor her, but sometimes…" Guy stood and walked to the ledger-laden table.

Laura stood and followed him, placing her hand on his shoulder. "It's hard?"

Turning, Guy's eyes searched her face.

"I feel the same way about my father. I'm trying to honor him, and I think I do, yet he keeps my wings clipped, which makes it hard to prove to him he has nothing to worry about. At least your mother helped you get a job at the bottom of the company and supported sending you here with the endorsement contract, which gave you a chance to prove yourself."

The gleam returned to Guy's eyes. The corners of his lips twitched into a smile. He turned and cupped his hands to Laura's cheeks. "Thank you. I never thought of it that way. You are such a special woman."

The appreciation in Guy's eyes combined with his touch torched her emotions, sending them into a blazing frenzy. He leaned his head closer.

The erratic beat of her heart resounded in her ears. The short shallow breaths she drew made her dizzy. No, not the breaths. Guy's nearness made her head spin faster than a lariat's loop. Unable to fight nature's pull, she leaned toward him. His cupped hand guided her face to his. Laura's eyes fluttered shut the moment his soft lips found their destination.

Time stilled to a slow lope. Joy burst through Laura. She savored Guy's tenderness. She lifted her hand to place it on his shoulder. He caught it with his free hand, placing it over his heart. The rapid drumming vibrated against her palm.

Guy ended the kiss. Laura opened her eyes. The depth of emotion shining from Guy's eyes matched what she felt inside.

"You have captured my heart." Emotion changed Guy's voice, made it lower and deeper.

The pitter-patter of Guy's heart grew more thunderous against her palm and matched her own in intensity.

"It doesn't seem logical in such a short time that I can feel so strongly for someone, but I do. Laura…"

I love you, too. A gasp wedged in Laura's throat at her heart's response. Love him? She didn't love him. She only spent time with him to ask business questions. Didn't she?

Chapter 12

"Laura." Guy cleared his throat to remove the heady emotion in his voice. Suddenly, Laura looked skittish as a scared horse.

A memory flashed through his mind. He fought the shiver of fear it produced. A horse didn't factor into the future he planned with Laura. He wanted—no, needed—to tell her how he felt so they could formulate a way to convince Jack a move to the city was best for his daughter.

"As I said, you've captured my heart. You returned my kiss, so I know you've developed feelings for me." Guy paused, giving Laura time to respond and his heart a chance to return to its normal rhythm.

Laura didn't respond. Instead, her eyes rounded. Her stony expression and lack of response whipped at his heart, causing it to beat faster.

Had he been wrong? Didn't she share his feelings?

He knitted his brows. Laura wasn't the kind of girl who kissed a man she wasn't interested in. "Laura, do you return my feelings?" Guy blurted out his question, which appeared to shock Laura out of her reverie.

She puckered her lips to the side. Her eyes searched his face. "I do, but…"

Pulling her hand free of his grasp, she clasped her hands and wrung them together. "You don't quite understand about my dream."

"Oh, but I do. We are kindred spirits, Laura, allowing our parents to guide our future."

"That's true." Laura's heavy breath wrung out her words, matching her twisting hands. A faraway look crossed through Laura's brown eyes. Was she contemplating Jack's reaction to this news?

Guy pulled her into a tight hug. "We need a chance to develop our relationship. We'll ask your father's permission together." Guy held her at arm's length and stared deeply into her eyes. "I'm sure he'll appreciate our honesty about this. I know I would. I value honesty."

A flicker of horror crossed Laura's face. Her body swayed in a small circle. He tightened his grip on her arms. He'd come on too strong. All of this was more than a fragile woman could take. He led her to the davenport. "I think you need to sit down."

She shook her head and lowered herself onto a cushion. Before Guy could offer her water or sit down beside her, a hard rap sounded at the door.

"I'll get it. Jack must have forgotten his key." When Guy answered the door, the desk clerk stood in front of it. "Here you are. Mr. Roberts, you have a visitor."

Guy looked around the doorframe. "Mother! What are you doing here?" Guy walked into his mother's outstretched arms and planted a polite kiss on her cheek.

"Hello, dear. I came with the amended contract."

"I thought you were mailing it."

"And pass up an opportunity to see an actual Wild West show? Not a chance. I can't let you have all of the fun."

Guy fought the urge to roll his eyes. Dodging horses wasn't fun.

"I know this isn't your suite. May I come in anyway?" His mother's raised brows indicated he'd forgotten his manners.

"Of course." Guy opened the door wide and stood back as his mother entered the room. He softly closed the door, then escorted her over to the davenport.

"Mother, this is Laura Barnes. Laura, this is my mother, Mrs. Roberts."

Laura stood and shook the hand his mother offered. "It's very nice to meet you, Mrs. Roberts."

"Likewise. Please call me Myrtle."

"We were just about to have coffee and cinnamon rolls." Guy pointed to the table. "Would you care to join us and tell us why you're really here?"

A sly smile stretched across his mother's lips. "He knows me too well. I am up to something. Mr. Turner decided to stage a publicity stunt to promote the endorsement between Papa Fizzy's and Buckskin Jones."

"What do you mean by a publicity stunt?"

There was no mistaking the wariness in Laura's voice or expression. Was she worried about her father or brother's reaction?

"I mean, we'll designate a day and time, throw a little party for the town, provide free samples of Papa Fizzy's Cream Soda and give them a glimpse of the Wild West show's costumes and attractions. Of course, we'll invite newspaper men from surrounding states so we can get lots of free press."

"Oh." A relieved smile lit Laura's face.

"Of course, Buckskin Jones and Starlight will make a personal appearance."

"Mother, do you really think this is wise—having a horse in a crowd of people?" Someone needed to keep their head about the risk and expense to the business. Giving away free soda pop would cut into their profit enough without having to pay for any injuries caused by a horse.

"Starlight would never hurt anyone." The incredulous look Laura shot Guy tightened his throat. He knew firsthand how a horse could injure people.

His mother pursed her lips and shook her head. "The horse will be there, son."

Laura turned a wide smile to his mother.

"It wouldn't look right for one of the stars of the show to not be there when the contract is signed."

In an instant Laura's wide smile faded. "What?"

Clapping her hands, his mother didn't seem to notice Laura didn't share her glee.

"The main draw of the event is Buckskin Jones signing the contract in person while the invited press snap pictures."

Laura's eyes rounded and the color drained from her face. "I don't think Dad's going to approve of this at all."

"I hate this." The whine in Pete's voice irked Laura even though it shouldn't. He was on her side and argued her point with their dad. They needed to come clean and tell the truth.

"This is fraud." Laura whispered through clenched teeth to her father.

"I know that." He snapped at Laura. His expression became contrite. He seldom lost his temper. "You both know for the past several days I tried everything I could think of to get out of doing this publicity stunt."

They stood huddled together on a corner of the town square waiting for Buckskin Jones's cue to ride down Main Street.

"Everything but telling the truth and crediting me with the act." Laura's raised voice startled Starlight. Her back legs danced a nervous jig. Laura tightened her grip on the horse's harness and gently patted her nose.

"We have been over this numerous times. Women who work in traveling shows are subjected to ridicule. Their reputations end up in tatters. I won't have anyone thinking that way about my daughter."

"I already work in a traveling show and my values haven't changed because you raised me to be a God-fearing woman. If a woman's reputation is ruined, it's because of her actions, not her occupation."

"That's not true, Laura. You have a good reputation because of your actions and the fact no one knows what your involvement in the show is."

Laura gulped. That wasn't true, either. She'd been careless and was certain she'd turned Clifford's suspicion to certainty. "I think Clifford knows."

"Harrumph. Clifford is too self-centered and arrogant to pay attention to another act. He doesn't know. He was here to steal the endorsement contract out from under us." Her father looked around. "What is taking so long?"

She and Pete watched their father tromp off in Guy's direction.

"I think he's worried." Pete turned to Laura. "You look real pretty in your outfit."

Starlight pulled against Laura's hold on the harness. "Thanks. I'm a little overdressed for a horse handler."

"Speaking of horses, what's wrong with Starlight today?" Pete patted the side of the paint's neck.

"Poor thing. She feels the tension, too."

"Mount up." Their dad rounded the corner of the building. "They're ready."

Laura gave the reins to Pete and continued to hold the harness tight while he mounted from the left. Once he was situated in the saddle, she made sure Starlight's harness was on straight so the stars made a straight line down the center of her nose.

Stepping back, Laura released the harness. Starlight skittered backward and sideways before Pete finally took control of her.

Her dad turned to her. "Shall we go and watch his entry?"

Laura's heart sank. She, not Pete, should be the one riding in to the applause of the small crowd of people. She shook her head. "You go on. I'll meet you by the stage."

"I'm sorry, Laura. You're young and someday you'll appreciate what I've done for you by protecting your reputation."

Her father did look contrite. She knew he had her best interest at heart and thought he was doing the right thing for her. He'd always encouraged her in her profession, bought her the horse she wanted. The only thing he didn't allow her to do was perform the act as herself. She gave her head a small nod, then watched her father walk away.

A man's voice boomed through a megaphone. The applause of the small crowd muffled the last part of his announcement. She heard enough to know it was Pete's introduction.

"I don't want to do this."

Laura looked up at Pete. "You have to." When he didn't spur Starlight, Laura slapped her rump hard. "Giddy-up, Starlight." She watched her horse carry Pete around the corner of the building and out of sight.

"I don't want you to, either," she whispered.

By the time Laura joined the festivities, the applause had died down. People sipped cream soda from bottles trickling with condensation. She walked over to her father and relieved him of Starlight.

"There you are!" Myrtle's voice and face reflected her mirth. "This turned out to be a well-attended event. And don't you look the part of a cowgirl in your pretty outfit? It's just darling. Why, you should be performing some type of act in the Wild West Extravaganza."

I do! This morning was harder than Laura had anticipated. Jealousy and hurt kept rearing their ugly heads. The polite conversation about her brother's riding ability irked her, making her answers clipped and slightly snotty. Laura swallowed hard before pasting a smile on her face and forcing silk back into her voice. "Thank you."

"Guy tells me you work behind the scenes at the show. You're the seamstress and enjoy designing the costumes."

Without thinking, Laura pursed her lips. She'd never had a chance to explain to Guy that he'd misinterpreted her dream.

"That's not true?" Myrtle's brows rose, matching the octaves of her voice.

"I sew costumes and our clothing. I don't think that

makes me a seamstress." She wanted to clarify at least one point.

Myrtle walked to the opposite side of Starlight and began to pet the horse's neck. "You have a calming effect on Starlight. She seemed a little antsy earlier with Pete, which is kind of odd, isn't it?"

Wariness niggled inside of Laura. Myrtle's question seemed to have a deeper meaning. It was like talking to Clifford. Or maybe it was her blue mood, reading more into what Myrtle said than perhaps the woman intended. Trying with all of her might, Laura kept her tone light with no hint of defensiveness. She hoped. "What do you mean by odd?"

"Oh." Myrtle waved her hand through the air. "I just meant they spend so much time together, you'd think they'd be at ease with each other." She shrugged her shoulders. "But maybe not. Guy said you exercise the horses, so maybe they're used to more than one handler."

Laura didn't get a chance to answer. The crowd's applause drew both women's attention to the area where Pete spun a lasso. With the loop close to the ground he jumped in and out of the spinning circle on one foot.

"It's about time for Pete to start signing autographs. Our photographer took a great action shot of him the other day. He's hanging from the side of the horse, his body parallel with Starlight's. What's that trick called?"

"The side drag."

"Of course the shot of his face isn't clear."

Air rushed from Laura's lungs. She tried to muffle the huffing sound but failed. Her heart pounded. Her instincts had been right; Myrtle's questions weren't innocent.

Myrtle gave her a concern-filled look. "Are you all right, dear?"

Laura didn't trust her voice. In fact, she didn't trust anything or anyone right now. She nodded her head. The burden of their family secret pressed down on her, putting another layer of negativity on her already disgruntled mood.

"Well, as I was saying, your brother is quite a talent—not only his showmanship, but he uses both hands equally, riding with his right and writing with his left. That's a talent few can master."

The bright smile Myrtle flashed in her direction didn't fool Laura. Myrtle knew Pete wasn't the Buckskin Jones performer.

Tears burned Laura's eyes. She blinked several times, trying to compose the emotions threatening to spill out of her and run down her face. She wished Myrtle would return to the crowd. Instead she cooed "good pony" into Starlight's ear while making long gentle strokes down the horse's neck.

Laura wanted to run away. Even though she wanted to honor her father, she was tired of lying and keeping secrets. Her gaze roamed the crowd of people gathered around Pete, heaping accolades on him that belonged to her. This day couldn't get worse.

"Ladies."

Clifford's twang caused Laura to lean against Starlight for support. Her mare twisted her head, rubbing her soft muzzle against Laura's shoulder. The little show of comfort was a balm for Laura's raw emotions.

She'd been wrong. The situation could get worse. "Clifford." Laura darted her gaze from the crowd to Clifford and then back.

"Laura."

For a few seconds silence surrounded them. Clifford cleared his throat. "Ma'am, I haven't had the pleasure to make your acquaintance. I'm Clifford Hutton."

The swinging fringe on the cuff of Clifford's bright blue shirt caught Laura's eye when he stuck his hand out. Where were her manners?

"I'm sorry. Mrs. Roberts, this is Clifford Hutton. Clifford, this is Guy's mother, Mrs. Roberts." By the charming look on Clifford's face, he already knew that. Had he come back to spill their secret and steal the endorsement contract?

"I thought he left town," Guy said to no one in particular. He watched Clifford's animated face from afar, as the showman tried to charm Laura and his mother.

"Don't let him bother you. He's a good person. A little career driven maybe." Jack stood with hands on his hips. "Let's stop the autograph party and get this contract signed."

Absently, Guy nodded. Something was wrong with Laura. He'd seen that horse twist its head around. Had she nipped Laura? He'd been subjected to the mean streak in his grandfather's steed, getting nipped or kicked any time he approached it. Icy fear shivered through Guy, although humidity dripped thicker than honey in the hot September sun.

"I agree." The sooner the horse was taken back to the fairgrounds, away from the crowd and Guy, the better.

Guy motioned for the trio to join the crowd while Jack extracted Pete from the autograph seekers.

"The photographer wants Pete sitting." Guy pointed to a small table draped with a white tablecloth sitting in front of a red brick building. "We want Starlight standing so it appears she's looking over his shoulder." Guy stiffened at the thought. A wild beast couldn't read. What a ridiculous pose! He drew several deep breaths. This stunt of his mother's couldn't end soon enough.

Coughs choked from him when Laura led Starlight past him. To allow for more than a few inches between him and the horse, he stepped back until he felt the rough brick biting into his jacket. Panic pressed down on him. His heart raced. He hadn't been this close to a horse since his grandfather's accident.

"Laura, don't lead the horse so close to people." Sweat beaded and trickled down the side of Guy's face.

Stopping and turning on her boot heel, Laura glared at Guy. "I know what I'm doing. Starlight is used to people, but she doesn't like tight spaces like this. Whose idea was it to put the table so close to the building? Even the most gentle and easygoing horse has some dislikes."

Starlight's hind legs danced, closing the space Guy carefully put between them. "Stop that." He directed his clipped words at the horse as he pressed back, flattening his body against the hard brick structure.

Laura narrowed her eyes. "I'm not doing anything."

Clifford's snicker drew Laura's angry gaze away from Guy. Guy didn't chance giving Clifford a look of his own. Guy kept his attention on Starlight's hind quarters, which never stopped moving.

The paint settled down when Laura got it into the position the photographer hoped for. Pete picked up the pen and had the first stroke of his name signed when the camera clicked.

Starlight's long, high-pitched whine echoed off the buildings just before she began to rise up. Horror widened Guy's eyes. Time stopped being fluid and jerked like a broken movie tape.

Laura scrambled to grab the reins and caught them.

Her low hold did nothing to stop the horse's rearing. Starlight's front legs pedaled the air.

"Mother, watch out! Laura, get hold of that beast before it hurts someone." Guy quickly moved away from the sturdy building.

The thump of Starlight's hooves on the ground reminded Guy of his grandfather's body falling. He closed his eyes. His body swayed at the memory of the horse rearing up, again and again, until his grandfather lost hold and whacked against the hard ground.

He opened his eyes. Laura held tight to the reins and patted the horse's neck. Guy surveyed the area. Everyone appeared unharmed and that was the way it was going to stay. It might not honor his mother, but he was going to take control of this situation. "Jack, Pete, take the horse away from the crowd before she hurts someone."

Fire blazed from Laura's eyes. "I can control Starlight."

"It's not a job for a woman." Guy turned to Pete.

Wide-eyed, Pete stood and tried to take the reins from Laura. Starlight pulled toward Laura and began to back away.

"Let go." Laura spat at Pete. "This is making her nervous."

"I said let Pete take care of his horse."

"Guy, you need to calm down." The warmth of his mother's hand on his shoulder did nothing to thaw the icy fear swirling inside of him.

"Mother, I've had enough of this crazy idea." Guy waved the reporters back a few feet before he picked up the contract and turned to Pete. "Pappy Fizzy's will offer you, as Buckskin Jones, an endorsement contact." He ripped the paper in two. "But not the horse."

"You can't do that." Laura came toward him, the horse trailing behind. She spoke so the crowd couldn't hear. "Starlight is a part of the act and deserves her moment in the spotlight. Besides, your company has invited all these reporters! What will it look like if you back out now?"

Guy looked to his mother for backup. A smug smile curled her lips. "Perhaps you're right, son. Mr. Barnes, I think we need to renegotiate this contract."

Laura's head snapped to his mother, then back. The forlorn look on her face stopped Guy's racing heart.

"Laura." He gentled his voice.

"Don't." Laura blinked rapidly.

"I'm sorry Starlight spoiled your publicity stunt." Jack's voice boomed. "We're willing to accept a contract without the horse."

"Dad, how could you?" Laura, reins in hand, swung into the saddle. With a flick of her heels, she and Starlight took off at a gallop down the street.

The silent crowd watched her ride away.

"Woo-wee." Clifford drawled. "Did you see that? Laura grabs the saddle horn with her right hand when she mounts Starlight, just like Buckskin Jones does." Then he turned to Pete. "But when you mount a horse, you use the crook of your right arm because of your weak right hand, don't you, Pete?"

Chapter 13

"Sit down and stop pacing." Guy's mother peered over her rimless glasses.

For a moment Guy stopped walking on the edge of the large square area rug in the spacious room his mother had rented for her stay. His fear had subsided. His heart no longer thundered in his chest or echoed in his ears, but he was far from calm.

Angry anxiety jittered through him until he took another step.

His mother's loud and exaggerated sigh bounced off the walls of the room. He took larger, faster steps. If she had listened to him in the first place, none of this would have happened. A wild horse had no business being in a throng of people. He knew it would add up to trouble and it had.

"What do you think Clifford meant?"

Guy stopped pacing and faced his mother. He wrinkled his brow. He remembered Clifford saying something right after Laura rode way. "His insinuation? I think he's trying to discredit the Barnes family and nab an endorsement contract for himself."

Turning away from his mother, Guy shook his head. He had noticed Pete's weak handshake. Would a hand injury cause him to compensate the way he mounted a horse? Guy rubbed his head. He'd been away from horses so long he couldn't be sure. There was one thing he was sure of, though—Clifford was trouble.

"Mother." Guy's abrupt turn wrinkled the heavy rug. "Clifford Hutton is an arrogant showman who is constantly making unwanted advances toward Laura. I thought when Jack didn't contract his act for the show it'd be the last we'd see of him."

A sly smile crept to his mother's lips. She slid her glasses down the bridge of her nose and took them off. "So you don't think Laura is Buckskin Jones?"

"The notion is preposterous." Guy threw his hands in the air. At first Clifford's statement this morning had given him pause. Then he realized Clifford's presence, and his fear clouded his mind, letting doubts replace rational thinking. The idea was illogical. Laura wasn't Buckskin Jones.

"All right." His mother held her hands in the air, palms out. "What should we do about the endorsement contract?" She lifted the torn legal document. Two vertical sheets of paper dangled in the air, proof his fear had forced him to act irrationally.

Guy marched over to the door. "I think we should offer them the original contract. I have it in my room. You heard Jack's verbal agreement. He said they'd accept it now." He reached for the knob.

"Not so fast."

He paused and turned at his mother's words.

She stood. "Something doesn't feel right to me. I recommend we search for another trick rider to endorse Papa Fizzy's Cream Soda."

"We can't." A sharp pang of fear twisted through Guy, wrapping around his heart and squeezing. He hated horses and the whole Western phenomena didn't appeal to him, but with Pete Barnes under contract with Papa Fizzy's, he'd have an excuse to see Laura.

"I think you should sit down, Guy. I believe you're still feeling the effects of your fright this morning. You look ashen."

Guy looked at his mother and blinked. Her face reflected her concern; however, her eyes held a glimmer of mischief.

He rubbed his forehead. This morning's incident muddled his mind. He needed to do something to clear it.

Work on the Western show's ledgers. That was another reason they couldn't pull the endorsement offer. The Barnes family worked hard to run an honest show, which needed an infusion of cash or this might be their last season.

"Mother, I'm fine. I just don't want to pull the endorsement contract away from the Barnes family."

"They've cost us a lot of money and time. And if you remember correctly, I wanted to sponsor a *girl* trick rider. Pete Barnes was your idea."

Guy fought the urge to sag under his mother's reminder. How his mother, a happy housewife, approved of working women was beyond Guy. "Mother, I stand behind my choice. I honored the company's wishes and came out here to place this endorsement contract.

I stayed for three weeks as requested. And now I want to try to finish the job."

"So you think Pete Barnes will still sign the contract?" His mother raised her brows. "After Laura made such a dramatic exit?"

"Laura wears her emotions on her sleeve. I believe she's a little high-strung due to her frustration over not fulfilling her dream." Guy fought to keep his voice under control. He didn't appreciate his mother's tone.

"Of being a seamstress?" If his mother lifted her brows any higher, they'd meet her hairline. Guy shook his head. Everyone seemed to be speaking in riddles today.

"Yes." Guy sighed. "I need to go talk to Laura. She loves her horse." Guy swallowed hard. "I have to explain to her why the beast shouldn't be included in the contract. Then I'm going to invite her to come to the city. Between our contacts, we should be able to help her realize her dream."

Guy started for the door.

"Just a minute. I'm coming with you."

Guy turned and watched his mother march across the room.

"You're a good girl." Laura cooed at Starlight as she pulled a brush through the short, coarse hair on the side of the mare's neck. "Don't listen to Guy."

Fresh tears burned Laura's eyes. What was wrong with him? Thinking Starlight was going to harm someone. She snorted her disbelief at the thought with each brush stroke. And why did she care what Guy thought of her or her horse anyway? "You didn't care for the hullaballoo any more than I did, did you, girl?"

"I should say not."

Laura stopped brushing Starlight, but she didn't look up. "I'm in no mood for your insinuations, Clifford. What are you doing back here anyway? Trying to steal our endorsement contract?"

"Nope. I got one of my own. A denim company." He chuckled. "Imagine all of the money I've spent on flashy costumes and they want to photograph me in my practice denims."

Relief replaced a little of the worry niggling at her mind. She turned. "Congratulations."

"Thanks."

"So why are you here?" Laura tipped her head. She'd never seen this earnest expression on Clifford's face before.

"Winona Phelps fell and broke her leg. I thought you might want to go to Colonel Cooper's and audition for her spot." Clifford removed his hat, and blond curls spilled down his face.

Laura's heart pounded hard. This was her chance. She needed to act on it. By the time she turned twenty-one, Winona's leg would be healed.

"Well?" Clifford searched her face. "You're still dressed in your fancy outfit. It will only take a few minutes to load Starlight into my truck. We'll be there in no time."

She bit her lower lip. Although she hated taking advantage of Winona's injury, she really wanted to go. Remorse harnessed her enthusiasm. Laura might not think Winona's act was up to par, but the accident could end Winona's career. *Lord, please relieve the pain in Winona's broken leg and help her bones heal properly. Amen.*

Her prayer reminded her of God and His commandments. She wanted to go, but that wouldn't be honoring her father. Besides, Papa Fizzy was still offering them the contract. It just didn't include Starlight. "Clifford, I don't know what you're talking about." Her words lacked conviction.

"Sure you don't." Clifford snorted. Walking up behind her, he removed the brush from her hand and tossed it to the ground. He placed his hands on her shoulders and stared straight into her eyes.

"Laura Barnes, I'm fond of you. I have been for a long time. When you're taken with a person, well, you notice things."

Laura's heart skipped, but not in the happy way Guy's touch brought. It was more of a panicked realization of what he'd say next.

"I've known for a long time there's a bigger trick than the back drag going on in your Western extravaganza. You're Buckskin Jones."

Tamping down her panic, she forced a laugh. "That's ridiculous."

The look Clifford pinned on her stopped her laughter. "No, it's not. You can fool the city dude, but you can't fool me. I know how important grip is while performing on the back of a horse. With Pete's bum hand, there is no way he could execute some of the tricks in your routine."

She shook her head. They'd been so careful. She'd designed twin buckskin suits. The wide-brimmed hat Buckskin Jones wore shaded her face.

"Laura." Clifford squeezed her shoulders. "I saw you practicing the signature trick, the back drag. I know you're Buckskin Jones."

Except for the purr of the engine of the Durant Star, the short ride to the fairgrounds was silent, which suited

Guy. He wanted to turn the situation over in his mind and formulate his plan. Laura wouldn't be happy about the removal of Starlight from the contract, but hopefully his offer to bring her to the city and help her find a seamstress position would counterbalance the situation like debits and credits in a ledger.

Knowing his mother wouldn't want to traipse through the pasture, Guy pulled into the fairgrounds entrance nearest to the arena despite the fact they were closer to the horses.

Once out of the car, Guy scanned the horizon for Laura. He saw her at the stables. The sun glimmered off her hair, playing with the color and turning the dark auburn a fiery hue.

He blinked. His heart clenched at the intimate way Clifford held Laura and looked down on her with affection. Jealousy poked at his heart, sharp and painful like the pointed tip of a freshly sharpened pencil piercing skin.

Without another thought for his mother, Guy marched through the trampled grass to where the two stood beside Starlight.

"What is going on here?"

Surprise registered on Laura's face. When their eyes met, she swallowed hard. Her hands jerked away from Clifford as if his arms had grown too hot to touch. Guilt washed over her features. She lowered her eyes. "It's not what you think."

Her words were barely audible over the hubbub around them. He turned to Clifford. "Remove your hands from Laura at once." Guy intended to step between them. No one was stealing the girl he loved away from him.

"This is none of your concern, city slicker." Clifford released one hand and started to pull Laura to him with the other. Guy knew the look of contempt Clifford shot his way was meant to intimidate him, but instead it fortified Guy. He stepped forward, intending to use physical force if necessary.

"Clifford, let go." Laura pushed her hands hard against Clifford's chest, breaking his hold.

"Did you come to apologize to me and Starlight?" Defiance flashed from Laura's dark irises. She planted herself between the two men, facing Guy. She squared her shoulders and set her jaw.

"I did not." Why would he apologize to a horse? "I came to tell you Mother is ready to pull the contract completely." Guy emphasized his last word. "However, I still feel Buckskin Jones and Papa Fizzy's are a good match. I've talked her into altering the contract back to its original form."

Laura fisted her hands and put them on her hips. "I don't think so. Starlight stays in our contract."

"Then I guess it's no contract." He hated to say those words after seeing their ledgers. Yet he couldn't let the company get trampled by a horse. A lawsuit could paralyze Papa Fizzy's or, even worse, force them to close their doors.

"I told you that you couldn't trust this city boy."

"I have had enough of you." Guy didn't appreciate Clifford's surly tone. He took a step toward him and felt his homburg lift from his head. Jerking his neck from side to side, the only person he saw was his mother and the only hat she had was the one on her head. Then someone or something nudged the center of his back, throwing him slightly off kilter.

He tensed. Every nerve in his body jittered. Righting himself, his breaths came quicker. Her horse was attacking him. He turned in time to see the ferocious beast's muzzle heading his direction again. He backed away.

"Don't just stand there and let that beast attack me." His voice, loud and shaky, sounded foreign and faraway, like a young boy calling for help.

Clifford's guffaws echoed through the pasture.

Guy looked to his mother for help and found her mouth twisting into a smile. "This is not a laughing matter. The beast tried to bite me."

"Guy." His mother stepped toward him. "I don't think you understand."

He held out a halting hand to his mother. "This is business and I'm handling this."

"Stop calling her a beast. She isn't going to hurt you." Laura's words snapped.

Starlight pushed her nose toward him, his hat clenched in her teeth. He wished he could pull his hat away, but his arm remained frozen to his side. He took a step back, stumbling over a clod of dirt. Starlight stepped forward. "Call off your horse and give me back my hat."

"Guy, the horse is trained to—"

Anger sparked through Guy at the way Clifford drawled out his name. "This is none of your business." Guy poked the air near Clifford's chest with his index finger. "You might as well leave. Papa Fizzy's will never offer you an endorsement contract, you vulture."

Clifford puffed his chest out and stepped toward Guy. "Why you…"

"Clifford, please leave."

The loud sigh Clifford heaved sounded like a horse's snort. Guy pursed his lips at the sparkle in Clifford's eyes when he looked at Laura. Jealousy's bitterness burned through him.

"Anything for you, Laura. Don't forget what we talked about." Clifford's devious smile and exaggerated wink heightened Guy's anger. He didn't like Clifford looking at Laura that way. Her brown eyes widened with fright. Obviously, she didn't like it, either.

With a fast swipe of her hand, Laura removed his hat from Starlight's teeth and held it out to him. "Here." She waved it in front of him.

"She ruined my hat." Guy snatched the hat from Laura and gave it a flip, which did nothing to remove the wet patch on the felt brim. "This is the reason the beast can't be in the contract. She's ruined my hat and she's going to hurt someone."

"She is not." Anger seared Laura's face until her skin was a perfect match for her hair. "You just don't know how to act around horses." Her eyes narrowed to slits, staring him down, daring him to continue the argument.

Laura's words pierced through his soul. They were true. Had he known how to act around horses, he might have been able to save his grandfather from a life of being wheelchair bound. His shame plus his fear added up to anger. Anger at Starlight. Anger at Laura. Anger at himself.

"My actions aren't in question. The horse's are. Papa Fizzy's can't take the risk of whether your horse will or won't hurt someone. Papa Fizzy's is going back to their original endorsement offer and that's final." Guy whipped his hat against his pant leg, turned on his heel and marched toward his car. "Let's go, Mother."

Chapter 14

Finally, Guy's heart beat at its normal pace. Running checks and balances on bookkeeping ledgers always calmed and relaxed him. He checked off the last number on the ledger page and placed the receipt in a neat stack.

He turned the page and noted the number at the top of a column. A deposit. He began to rummage through the box, looking for the deposit ticket to match the amount.

Had Laura calmed down? Absently, Guy ran his fingers through the papers in the box. He hated the fact they quarreled over something as trivial as adding a horse to a contract. He hated leveling the ultimatum. He hated knowing that once the contract was signed he'd have to go back to the city.

Guy stopped rummaging through the papers. He hadn't thought about occupying the corner office, running the accounting department at Papa Fizzy's or investing in the stock market for quite some time.

Working with the Barnes family had allowed him to see business from a variety of angles, watching auditions, setting up concessions and tackling simple book work.

Well, the book work would be simple once he got their ledgers in shape. Verifying the number, Guy began to look through the receipts, sorting them in piles by company. In minutes Guy emptied the box. All of the deposit tickets sat in a neat stack. Not one matched the entry in the lined ledger. Not one matched the date, either.

He needed a bank statement to verify the numbers. He'd have to ask Jack for it later. Moving down to the next entry, Guy ran his finger across the line. He needed a receipt from the feed company. He lifted the stack and thumbed through them.

His mind wandered to Laura. Hurt pressed his heart. He shouldn't have walked off that way. He should have stayed and reasoned with her, explained the legal aspects of having Starlight on the contract. He should have stayed calm and rational.

What was that? A number caught his eye. He flipped the receipt back over. Guy rubbed his eyes. He held the paper closer to the window. He couldn't believe it, but it was true. The number on the feed receipt matched the deposit figure.

Guy's shoulders sagged. The possibility of a transposed number had crossed his mind but not the transposition of a deposit and withdrawal. He quickly leafed through the deposit tickets and found the deposit that matched the feed entry. A credit and debit had been reversed.

His involuntary sigh cut through the room. The correction would put the Western show in the red. They needed this endorsement. Guy rubbed his eyes again, and his fingertips brushed his forehead. He hoped the removal of Starlight didn't sway Pete's decision to sign the legal document.

He liked the Barnes family, especially Laura. He saw a future with her, wanted a future with her. He shook his head. It wasn't logical. In four short weeks people couldn't fall in love, yet he had fallen for Laura and thought she felt the same way.

Could he be wrong? From a distance her actions with Clifford that afternoon had an intimate feel. Did she and Clifford have a secret relationship? They had a lot in common. Similar backgrounds. A love of horses.

Guy shivered. Two things he didn't share with her. They did have things in common, though. Their respect for their parents. Their Christian beliefs. The heaviness on Guy's heart pressed harder. He needed to speak to Laura.

Standing, Guy slipped on his jacket. He wiggled his shoulders and tugged at the sleeves to ease the tweed's confinement. He missed the comfort of his Western-cut shirt. He'd check at the front desk to see if they'd seen her walk through the lobby or go into the restaurant.

Fear caught in his throat. He swallowed hard. He'd return to the fairgrounds if he had to.

After searching the hotel for her with no results, he did have to return to the fairgrounds. He mustered his courage and searched the area for Laura. When he didn't find her, he stood beside the bleachers and watched Pete work with a horse in the corral.

Pete wore a fedora and stood with his back to Starlight. The horse came up behind him and removed the hat, then bunted Pete's back with its muzzle. Pete faked a stumble and did a somersault. The worker's children sitting on the bleachers giggled. Pete stood, scratched his head and turned back to the horse. He held his hand out for his hat. The horse shook its head. The air chimed with the children's laughter.

Guy smiled. By the end of the act, when the horse set the hat back on Pete's head, Guy laughed harder than the children.

"Now you know what was so funny earlier this afternoon."

Guy was startled. He hadn't heard Laura come up behind him.

"I…um…didn't realize." Suddenly his collar felt too tight. He pushed two fingers between the fabric and his neck and pulled a little. It didn't help.

"It was part of an act. Clifford tried to tell you. Your mother realized it."

Guy dropped his head.

"Why are you afraid of horses?"

Laura's question held no condescension.

Guy's chest bounced as he drew in a ragged breath. "When I was eight I witnessed a horse attack my grandfather. The stallion seemed massive when it reared up and towered over Grandfather." Emotion shook Guy's voice. "Grandfather stood his ground, reins in hand. The horse twisted and Grandfather lost his grip on the reins. The momentum knocked him off balance. He fell to the ground on his hands and knees. Before he could get up the untethered horse brought its front legs down on Grandfather's back." Guy stopped and fought the shudder of fear in the pit of his stomach. The thwack of the stallion's hooves on his grandfather's back still resounded in his ears.

He closed his eyes. "I should have moved, done something to divert the horse's attention. It was so big and ominous." Guy hadn't realized he'd spoken out loud until he felt the warmth of Laura's touch.

"Some horses are temperamental. Some are gentle. Starlight is a gentle horse."

Guy opened his eyes. Trust and love beamed from Laura. Was it for him or Starlight?

"Give me your hand and I'll show you." Laura motioned Guy over to the fence. She clicked her tongue. Starlight obeyed Laura's cue and came to the fence, hanging her muzzle over the top board.

Fear trembled his palm, but he managed to hold it out to Laura. When she cupped his hand in hers, his knuckles grazed her soft skin. His hand continued to shake even cradled in Laura's steady hold. Slowly, she guided their hands to Starlight's muzzle.

Pull back. His arm muscle tensed under his desire to give into his fear. He looked at Laura. The gentleness in her eyes and slight jerk of her head toward Starlight urged him on.

Starlight lifted her nose and dropped her muzzle into his open palm. The silky flesh tickled his skin while a gentle tongue flicked across his fingers in search of a treat.

"See, she's a good girl. She'd never hurt anyone. She reared up today because she sensed tension." Laura dropped her hand from his. Starlight continued to rest her muzzle in his hand.

"Isn't that the softest thing you've ever felt?" The sun caught the sparkle in Laura's eyes. She ran her thumb over the hairless skin around Starlight's nostrils and mouth.

"No." Guy swallowed hard. He caught Laura's fingers in his. "This is." He brought her hand to his lips, placing a whisper of a kiss on each knuckle.

"Oh!"

When Guy lifted his eyes to Laura's face, her lips curved into a soft smile. Guy stood in disbelief. He was actually inches from a horse. "Laura, I'm sorry about our quarrel this afternoon. Can you forgive me?"

"Yes, and now you see Starlight is one of God's gentle creatures."

"I do." Guy glanced at Starlight. All these years he'd measured every horse by the stallion that injured his grandfather. "I've been wrong about most horses for a long time."

Laura beamed with happiness.

Guy touched Starlight's muzzle again and continued to stroke her soft face. He still felt a little nervous around her, but he was beginning to see how he had overreacted to many situations. It was time to conquer his fear and move on. Maybe if he got used to Starlight he could get used to other horses, as well. If horses were part of Laura's life, they'd have to be part of his, too.

He turned to Laura and took her hand. "Laura, in the short time we've known one another I've developed strong feelings for you. I think you return them, yet this afternoon with Clifford…" Guy allowed his voice to trail off when jealousy gripped his throat. He didn't want this moment to be ruined by accusing tones.

Clearing his throat, he continued. "This afternoon your conversation appeared to be quite intimate. I'm just wondering…"

Laura's smile turned to a slight grimace. "My relationship with Clifford is strictly business." Laura's eyes darted around the pasture while the toe of her red boot rapidly tapped up and down.

"Is something wrong?" Guy wrinkled his brow.

"No, no, nothing is wrong." Laura's words didn't match the guilty expression on her face.

"You have no interest in Clifford."

"None." Laura spoke the word with no hesitation.

Guy smiled. "Do you have an interest in me?" Nerves shook his voice.

She dropped her eyes, then lifted them, locking her gaze with his. "I do."

"I think it could be love." Guy's voice turned to a low whisper.

"Me, too."

Her admission lifted his confidence. Happiness burst through him. He squeezed her hand. "That's wonderful. Once we get this contract signed, I'm going to speak with your father. Mother and I want you to come to Sioux City with us. We have a spacious home, and you can stay with us. Mother and I have many contacts in the garment industry. I am certain you'll be living your dream within a month's time."

Astonishment squeaked from Laura. Hope shined in Guy's eyes. She broke their stare, focusing her gaze over Guy's shoulder and letting it settle on Starlight. She wished she could clear up this misunderstanding. Tell Guy the truth. She was Buckskin Jones and her dream was to drop the character and continue trick riding. It was not to be a seamstress.

Telling Guy the truth wouldn't be honoring her father, though, would it? She was so tired of living a lie. Fooling the audience was one thing. Many performers took on different personas. Pete did when he performed his comedy routine. But not being completely honest with Guy and Myrtle in this endorsement contract was nothing short of lying.

Relief washed through her at the realization that Pete hadn't signed the contract. It was a good thing Starlight had reared up during the press conference. Maybe there was still time for them to tell the truth. After all, Myrtle had indicated she wanted to have a girl trick rider sponsor their soda pop.

With a slight movement, Laura rested her eyes on Guy. *He* didn't want a girl trick rider, though. Not to endorse their product or for a potential wife. Her heart dropped. Despite his opinions of horses and a woman's place in society, she did care for him. Deeply. How could that be?

"I know you need time to think about this move. I plan to speak to Jack. Tell him Mother runs a good Christian home and would chaperone us during our courting period."

Laura managed a smile. "I couldn't leave. Dad needs me to help him with the show." She'd never audition for Colonel Cooper. She'd stay here with her family. She'd pray Clifford respected her wishes and her family enough that he'd keep their secret. Her heart wrenched. What if he didn't?

She hung her head and looked at her costume. She hadn't been careful enough with it. Two men saw it and jumped to different conclusions. One was right, the other wrong.

Guy's fingers lifted her chin. "Don't worry. This will all work out."

Laura looked into eyes filled with love and trust. Her heart sank further in her chest. She hung her head.

"I'm going to find your father." Guy chucked her chin until she raised her eyes to his. "This will all work out. I promise."

Thank goodness Guy insisted on leaving to find her

father. Laura petted Starlight's side and watched him walk away. She slipped an arm around the mare's neck and leaned her head against it. The coarse hair and familiar scent comforted Laura.

"What a mess I'm in. What am I going to do, girl?" Laura squeezed Starlight's neck tighter. The horse twisted around and nudged Laura with her muzzle. "That *is* a good idea." Laura loosened her hold and patted Starlight's neck.

Resting her arms on the horse's back, she clasped her hands and bowed her head. *Dear God, please show me the right thing to do. I've tried to honor my father by doing what he asked with the trick-riding routine, but it doesn't feel right anymore. It feels like lying. I don't want to mislead Guy and Myrtle. How can I convince Clifford not to tell our competition about our ruse? Please guide me in the way that is pleasing to You. Amen.*

Tears formed at the corners of Laura's eyes. She swiped them away with the back of her hand. She walked through the pasture to the road leading to town. Her father had done such a fine job raising her and Pete after their mother passed away. Why didn't he trust them to prove that they were honorable people? Following in Winona Phelps's footsteps and tarnishing her reputation was the furthest thing from Laura's mind. She just wanted to use her God-given talent and receive the accolades for it.

After all, someday she did want to marry and have children of her own. An image filled her mind of red-haired children with Guy's deep blue eyes.

Beep, beep, beep. Laura's body jerked. She'd been so lost in thought. Had she veered into the road? The purr of an engine slowed. She looked over, intending to apologize for being in the way.

"Are you coming with me?" Clifford stopped his truck. He leaned over his steering wheel and called out the open passenger window.

"No." Laura gripped the edge of the window. She saw hurt and disappointment in Clifford's blue eyes. "Are you going to tell everyone about our act?"

He turned his head and looked out the windshield.

Laura's heart pattered in rhythm with the chug of the truck engine as she waited for his answer.

Clifford turned back to her. His lips drew into a grim line. He shook his head. "Naw. It's just part of the business. I wish you'd come with me, though. You deserve to have top billing, Laura. You're a good trick rider."

Clifford's praise caused fresh moisture to spring to Laura's eyes. "Thanks."

"I don't know what a cowgirl sees in a city fella." Clifford gave a snort, then smiled. "I'm hanging around the fairgrounds for another hour, if you have a change of heart."

"I won't." Laura smiled. "Goodbye." She backed away from the pickup and waved as Clifford slowly pulled off.

She started walking. Her smile widened with the knowledge Clifford wasn't going to spill their secret. Then she thought about what he'd said. *It's part of the business.* Putting on an act is part of the business. If Papa Fizzy's wanted to do business with the Wild West Extravaganza, then they needed to understand that part of the business, too.

She'd agree to any endorsement terms as long as Guy and Myrtle understood who suited up in buckskin and performed the tricks. Although her stomach flip-flopped, she planned to find Guy and tell him the truth.

By the time Laura reached the hotel, her steps became determined even if her legs shook and her pulse thundered in her ears. She didn't know how Guy would take this news. She did know how she'd feel. Better.

Laura headed to their suite to change out of her Western outfit. Muffled voices greeted her at the door. Slowly she turned the knob and peeked in. Her father, Pete, Myrtle and Guy sat around the table, passing a piece of paper back and forth. The endorsement contract?

"Are you signing the endorsement contract?"

Pete nodded his head.

"Why wasn't I included?" Laura frowned. Pete hung his head. Her gaze flew to her father.

Chair legs scraped against the worn wooden floorboards. Guy stood. "It's best to leave business to men."

Anger, sudden and strong, flooded through her. "Your mother's here. She's a woman."

Guy crossed his arms and gave her a pointed look. "True. Perhaps both of you should go downstairs to the restaurant and have a cup of tea."

Laura watched Guy turn to his mother for a show of support. The hopeful expression he wore faded to surprise when he met an icy glare instead.

"You are not dismissing us, are you?" Myrtle made no show of moving from her chair.

"I think it's a nice way to spend the afternoon." Jack stood, creating a unified front for Guy.

Myrtle quirked an eyebrow at the men. "What do you think, Laura?"

"I want to stay." Laura stared up at her father, who gave her a slight headshake. Twenty-four hours ago,

Laura would have honored her father's cue and left the room. Not today. Papa Fizzy's needed to know who they were endorsing, who Buckskin Jones really was. She looked into her father's eyes. "I plan to stay."

"Really, Laura, this doesn't concern you."

Laura narrowed her eyes at the firmness in Guy's voice.

"Laura, come with me." Her father placed his hand on her elbow and guided her to the corner of the room by the table housing their ledgers.

"How could you leave me out of this meeting?" She spat the words out in a whispered huff.

"Because you want to keep changing the conditions of the contract. I allowed it before, but I can't now. We *need* this endorsement. Guy found a bookkeeping error. The show is in trouble." Jack ran his fingers through his hair and stared at the books.

"Dad." Laura angled herself so her father blocked her view to the others. "Make me, not Buckskin Jones, the headliner. Girl trick riders bring in a bigger crowd. With my signature trick, we'll sell more tickets. Tell Guy and his mother the truth, and they'll still offer the endorsement contract. I know they will."

She watched her father's expression change as he considered her whispered plea. Sadness veiled his eyes. "I can't, Laura. I can't lead you into a life of temptation that will ruin your reputation."

"But it won't." Laura blinked rapidly to hold back her tears.

Her dad glanced over his shoulder, then back at her. "If you promise to keep quiet and let Pete sign the endorsement contract, you can stay in the room."

Chapter 15

Laura drew a ragged breath, hoping to steady her anger and control her tears before she nodded.

"Laura's going to stay." Her dad pointed at the davenport before resuming his place at the table.

"She'll feel left out way over there." Myrtle took turns looking at the men around the table. When her gaze settled on her son, he stepped aside.

"You may have my chair, Laura."

She managed a polite grin before slipping onto the pressed cardboard seat.

"Let's get Laura up to speed on the endorsement contract." Myrtle smiled warmly at Laura.

Guy walked around the table and stood behind his mother. "We are going back to the original endorsement offer for Pete Barnes, alias Buckskin Jones. Starlight will not be included."

The remorseful look Guy gave her seemed sincere.

"However, we are going to increase the amount of the endorsement figure by two hundred dollars and plan to bring more exposure to Papa Fizzy's Cream Soda and Wild West Extravaganza by lining up personal appearances for Buckskin Jones throughout the Midwest."

Hurt tromped Laura's heart. She pressed it down and forced a smile. Her father reached over and patted her hand.

"Although—" Myrtle tipped her head from side to side "—I've decided we need a close-up picture of Buckskin Jones performing the back drag. That's his signature move, right? The one no other trick rider performs?"

"Yes. That's his move. It'd be mighty hard to get a close-up shot of that." Her father's chuckle boomed through the room. "I'm not trying to be difficult. You're being more than generous, but we can't agree to that photograph."

"Why not?"

Myrtle's sugared tone sounded a little too innocent to Laura, especially after their conversation at the publicity stunt.

Laura tried to catch her father's eye and give him some sort of cue to indicate that Myrtle was on to their antics. Unfortunately, her father's eyes were on Guy as he continued disputing Myrtle's wishes. "It's just not feasible. How can a camera catch a moving shot without blurring the photo?"

"A regular camera can't. A movie camera can and then they will freeze the shot I want and make a photo."

"Mother, that'd be quite expensive. I don't think Mr. Turner would approve." Guy's scolding tone drew Myrtle's mouth into a frown. "This is why women aren't consulted in business."

"Guy, are you implying that women haven't any business sense?"

Pulling on his shirt collar, Guy's Adam's apple bounced. "Yes, Mother, that's exactly what I'm saying."

"Mr. Barnes, do you agree with Guy?"

"I do."

"Pete, how do you feel about my idea?"

Had it been a different situation, Laura might have giggled. Now she hoped Myrtle didn't notice. Pete had nodded off. Pete's head popped up. He blinked his eyes.

"If Laura likes it, I like it."

"Well, Laura what do you think?" Myrtle's smile grew sly.

"I think showing the back drag in ads might give away the excitement of the show." Laura chose her words carefully. There was no way to take a picture of the pose without giving away their ruse.

"I hadn't considered that. Then we'll change it to another posture." Myrtle clicked her fingers and looked at Pete. "The one where you're on the side hanging parallel to the horse."

Pete could probably perform the trick, but it'd be from the opposite side Laura performed it. Would Guy and Myrtle notice? Laura peered at Pete. He shot her a panicked look.

"Oh, and you'd need to hold a bottle of Papa Fizzy's Cream Soda."

Laura choked. Pete didn't have the grip for that.

"Are you all right, dear?"

Laura nodded her head.

"So we agree on the shot for the photo?"

"No, holding the bottle of soda puts Pete in danger. He needs to have a free hand." Her father crossed his arms over his chest as he shook his head.

"Well, if something goes wrong, he can drop the bottle of soda to the ground. We'd understand. His safety comes first."

"Mother, let's keep the original idea for the publicity shot. A headshot of Buckskin Jones holding a bottle of Papa Fizzy's. Not only is it safer, it's also cheaper."

Myrtle wiggled her head from side to side again in consideration. "No, I want Buckskin Jones doing a trick and holding a bottle of cream soda."

Pete's boot tapped against Laura's. She looked at her brother. His eyes pleaded with her. He knew he couldn't do what Myrtle asked, but he'd never go against their dad's wishes. Laura cast a sideways glance at her father, then looked Myrtle directly in the eye.

"Pete would pose in the trick-riding stance you're suggesting if he could—" Laura gulped "—but he can't because I'm Buckskin Jones."

"What?" Guy's voice boomed through the room.

Cringing, Laura drew her gaze from Myrtle's satisfied expression to Guy's horror-filled one.

"When Buckskin Jones is in the arena performing tricks for the crowd, it's me. Me, not Pete."

"Laura, that's enough." The stern tone of her dad's voice was a clear indication to stop talking.

She refused to take his cue. "It's not enough. If we are going to sign the endorsement contract, they need to know the truth. I am the trick rider. Pete is the front man."

Bitter tears burned Laura's eyes.

"How could you have lied to me?" Appalled at her admission, Guy's cobalt eyes darkened. Gone was the sparkle of love. "You know how I feel about girl trick riders."

He might have been asking all of them, but his eyes bore down on Laura.

I've lost his love. She knew there was a chance of that when she told the truth. Still she felt the need to explain, maybe win his love again. Guy was thoughtful and logical. Surely he'd forgive her and understand why she hadn't told him sooner. "I'm sorry you were mistaken about my dream. My dream is to be a trick rider on my own terms."

"You never corrected me." Guy paced to the center of the room.

Laura scooted away from the table and stood. "I couldn't. I was honoring my father by doing what he asked me to do, which involved keeping Buckskin Jones's true identity a secret."

Facing her, Guy's features twisted with revulsion where love had once shone.

Her heart squeezed so tight she lost her breath. She glanced over her shoulder at her family and back at Guy before she ran from the room.

Taking the stairs two at a time, she stopped briefly at the front desk. Her tears dotted the paper as she scratched out a note to her father, pushed it toward the desk clerk, darted out the hotel door and ran toward the fairgrounds.

"Pfst…pfst…pfst…" Guy sputtered. His chest heaved, yet he couldn't catch his breath. *His* Laura performed dangerous stunts on a horse.

He looked at the faces around the table, yet didn't really see them. Instead, the clues he missed during his month stay began to add up. Laura's aggravation at his praise for Pete's riding abilities, her graceful posture, the buckskin practice suit, her leg injury, the Barneses' hesitancy to sign the endorsement contract in front of a crowd of people and Starlight responding to Laura's, not Pete's, commands.

"You've made a fool of me." Anger burned in his tone. He turned to Jack Barnes. "I thought you ran an honest family business exactly like Papa Fizzy's. We were a perfect match for a business partnership. This changes everything." Guy grabbed the endorsement contract from the table.

"Don't rip that contract in two." His mother's sharp words stopped his wrist midflick.

Surprise flashed through Jack's eyes. "You're pulling the endorsement contract? It's still the same act, just not a male rider."

Anger shot up Guy's back, pulling him ramrod straight. "I don't do business with dishonest people."

Jack stood. "We're not dishonest. I was protecting my daughter's reputation."

"Protecting your daughter?" The question boomed through the room. "By allowing her to perform dangerous tricks on a ferocious beast? What kind of father allows his precious daughter to do a man's work?" The volume of his voice rose with each question. "I saw the mark left on her leg by Starlight's hoof. A foot higher and your beautiful daughter would be confined to a wheelchair for the rest of her life, like my grandfather."

"Guy, your grandfather's horse was startled." Myrtle rose from her chair and walked over to him. She placed her hand on his shoulder. "The horse didn't purposely attack your grandfather. It was an accident. He fell and the horse stepped on him."

"Trampled him, mother, trampled him. I was there." Bitter tears stung Guy's eyes even after all of these years.

"Yes, the horse trampled him, but it was an accident and you were a little boy. You couldn't have prevented it." She squeezed his shoulder. He looked into her loving eyes and thought of Starlight's gentle affection earlier in the day. It had been an accident. The horse didn't intentionally harm his grandfather. His rational mind finally reconciled the memories of a scared little boy.

Clearing his throat, he glared at Jack. "This changes nothing. I'm not offering a contract to a girl trick rider."

"And why not?" His mother stood back and crossed her arms over her chest.

"Because my daughter isn't ruining her reputation," Jack said. "I've seen how women performers act once they get in the limelight." He shook his head.

Guy's mother pulled a face at Jack's comment. "Laura seems to have a good head on her shoulders. Why do you think she'd change if you let her perform in her flashy outfit?"

Jack's shoulders sagged. "I don't know."

"Well, it seems to me you've raised her right, except for the Buckskin Jones scam."

"I guess you could be right."

After an eye roll, Guy's mother turned to him. "And explain to me why you don't want a pretty girl to endorse our product?"

"A woman's place is running the home front, the way you do. It's not running a business."

"Is that so?" His mother raised her eyebrows.

She glanced at Jack before pursing her lips. "Guy, I believe offering the endorsement contract to Laura would increase per unit sales, which increases our profit margin on our income and expense report."

Guy's mouth gaped. "How do you know that?"

His mother's sigh cut through the room. "Jack's show

isn't the only scam in town. I easily figured out the Buckskin Jones ruse because I've done the same thing since your grandfather died. I run Papa Fizzy's."

"What?" Guy threw his hands in the air.

"You heard me. Your father knew and approved right up until the day he died. He came up with my alias."

"Mr. Turner?" Guy rubbed his temples. Why wasn't life black and white like lead on paper? "Why didn't you tell me?"

"For reasons similar to Jack's. Most men feel exactly the way you two do about women in the workforce. They are either ignored or their reputation is besmirched."

Disbelief coursed through Guy. Did he only see what he wanted to see in life? "Were all of your social engagements really business meetings?"

His mother nodded her head. He'd reviewed the company's income and expense reports over the past ten years. The business became more successful after Mr. Turner—no, his mother—took over the company. Guy opened his mouth ready to ask the next question when someone tapped on the door.

Pete jumped to his feet and ran to the door like a scared rabbit looking for cover. He threw it open, no doubt hoping Laura had returned. It was the desk clerk.

"I have a note for Jonathan Barnes."

"It's in Laura's handwriting." Pete slipped the paper from the desk clerk's hand and absentmindedly closed the door.

In an instant, Jack stood beside Pete. He opened the paper and studied it for a long time.

"What does it say?"

"She's run off with Clifford."

"What?" Guy moved close to the two men. His heart squeezed tight in his chest.

"To audition for Colonel Cooper's show," Jack slapped the paper hard against his palm.

"Dad, what are we going to do? We need Laura." Pete began to pace.

"If you want an endorsement contract from Papa Fizzy's, you do need Laura. I want a girl trick rider to endorse our cream soda."

Guy could tell his mother's firm tone didn't allow for argument.

The low afternoon sun burned hot through the windshield of Clifford's pickup. The humid breeze coming through the rolled-down side window did little to cool Laura's skin.

She fanned her face with her hand. The first hour of the drive, her hurt and anger supported her decision to leave the Wild West Extravaganza. Once the anger started to fade, doubt niggled at her mind. Without Buckskin Jones, her father's show didn't have a chance of survival. Maybe she should ask Clifford to take her back home.

She glanced at Clifford. If word got out about the trick the Barneses pulled on the public, the rumor could ruin the show, too. She stopped fanning her face and rubbed her temples. She sure wasn't honoring her father now.

All she ever wanted was for her talent to be acknowledged. She inhaled deeply and held the sigh inside. Laura closed her eyes. Guy's handsome face twisted into a horrified expression and her father's look of shock rotated through her mind. Both men said they cared for her, yet they didn't believe in her. God gave her the ability to be a talented trick rider and she had to go through with this audition to prove it to them. She'd show her father that her morals and convictions couldn't be swayed. She'd show Guy a woman wasn't a fragile piece of china to be kept on a kitchen shelf.

"How much longer until we get to Colonel Cooper's practice site?" Laura turned in her seat.

"Why? Are you having second thoughts?" Clifford cast a sideways glance her way.

"No, the opposite. I'm anxious." Laura looked out the back window at Starlight riding in the high-sided pickup box. "Do you think he'll want me to audition right away? Starlight will need some exercise after this long ride."

"I'm sure if he's not busy, he'll let you audition."

For a few seconds Laura fidgeted with her fingers. "If he doesn't hire me and Starlight, will you take me back to Dad's show?"

Clifford glanced her way, a smirk creasing his face. "You are the only trick rider who's brave enough to do a back drag. He'll hire you. Why don't you get some shut-eye?"

When the truck slowed and bounced through ruts in a gravel road, Laura opened her eyes. Bursts of purplish hues hovered over the horizon, bidding farewell to the sun. She stretched.

"Almost there." Clifford guided his truck around a bend.

Shiny red fencing surrounded freshly turned soil. Three bleacher sections, with matching painted boards, lined the side of the fence. The few hands milling around the arena wore blue jeans and red Western shirts.

As soon as Clifford stopped, one of the hands approached the pickup and started dropping the end gate to unload Starlight.

Clifford opened his door. "This is your chance. Here comes Colonel Cooper now." He pointed.

An older gentleman dressed in flashy attire similar to Clifford's walked straight toward the vehicle. Laura unlatched the door and slid from the seat.

"Colonel Cooper." Clifford met the man at the front of the truck. "This is the girl trick rider I told you about, Laura Barnes. Laura, this is Howard Cooper."

Laura shook the Colonel's hand. "You Jack Barnes's daughter?"

Guilt shivered through her. "Yes."

"That's good enough for me. I'll give you a few minutes to get the traveling kinks worked out, then you can show me what you've got." With a quick nod, he strode away.

Laura scowled at the brusque treatment. Her dad always took the time to get to know the people who auditioned for him.

"You'd better get a move on." Clifford jerked his head toward Starlight. "I'll be watching in the bleachers."

It took Laura fifteen minutes to get Starlight saddled and warmed up and her nerves under control. This was what she dreamed of, wasn't it? Her heart sank. It was her dream to perform in her red leather Western outfit. But not here; she wanted to work for their family business, help it prosper the same way Guy dreamed of doing for Papa Fizzy's.

She'd made a mistake coming here. However, she'd given Clifford and Colonel Cooper her word and she had to honor it. It was the way her dad had raised her. Sucking in a deep breath, she led Starlight over to the arena gate.

She nodded to a hired hand, and he opened the gate. Laura sucked in a deep breath and tapped her legs against Starlight. Together they galloped into the arena. Forcing a smile, Laura opened her act by waving to the crowd, about twelve hands who sat on the bleachers. After one loop around the arena, Laura began the first trick, the Cossack drag. Hanging upside down over the side of the horse, the world blurred.

Gracefully, she righted herself and took a breath before performing the cartwheel trick. As the small crowd applauded, she twisted around and began to get ready for the next posture. She almost missed putting her foot in the crupper handle, the extra stirrup on the saddle. Her vision came back in line. Leaning over the fence was Guy and Myrtle, Pete and her dad.

She froze. Holding on to the saddle horn she rode around the arena again. When she passed by the group, her father cupped his hands around his mouth. "Do your routine."

A genuine smile creased her face. Guy stuck a thumb up in the air and her vision blurred. Tears, happy tears, sprang to her eyes. She could tell by their faces, they were proud of her. Waving to the crowd again, Laura completed the trick she'd started. She completed her routine with precision. Finally positioning her legs in the special stirrups on the saddle, she flipped over the back of Starlight, letting her arms dangle by Starlight's tail.

Whoops and shouts, clapping hands and whistles erupted as Starlight galloped in the wide arena circle. Pulling herself up, she secured her footing and lifted into the hippodrome, hands held high and waving.

Slipping back into the saddle, she rode through the arena opening. She stopped Starlight and dismounted.

The small crowd of people who'd watched the audition headed her way, led by her father and Guy.

Laura braced for the two men's disappointment Myrtle pushed through between them, reaching her first. She wrapped Laura in a hug. "You were wonderful."

"Yes, you were." Laura's eyes widened at her father's remark. "Laura, I'm sorry I forced you do something you didn't want to do. You are an excellent trick rider and deserve headline billing. If you come back to our show, that's what you'll get. No more character gimmicks. And I'll trust you'll never change or become brazen."

Laura wrapped her father in a tight hug. "Thank you, Dad."

Guy cleared his throat. Laura released her embrace on her father. She turned to face the man she respected and loved, even if he no longer returned those feelings.

"I'm sorry I misled you about my dream. This is my dream. I know Papa Fizzy's doesn't want to endorse a woman trick rider, but I'm never pretending to be someone else again. If I perform, I perform as me." She looked into Guy's cobalt eyes, unable to read the emotion running through them.

"Laura, I was wrong to feel that way. Today I learned that a woman can manage more than a household." Without warning, Guy stepped forward and wrapped his arms around her. "You are a fantastic trick rider and Papa Fizzy's is ready to offer you an endorsement contract."

She leaned into the warmth of his embrace and looked up into his sparkling blue eyes.

"I love you, Laura Barnes."

Laura looped her arms around his neck and whispered in his ear. "I love you, too."

The clap of Myrtle's hands broke their embrace. "It's settled then. We'll draw up a new contract for a three-year endorsement deal with Laura Barnes and Starlight."

"No, Mother, we won't. I disagree with the offer."

Laura gasped. Her heart twisted in her chest.

"The contract for Laura Barnes and Starlight should only be for one year. One year is a long enough courting period." Guy's face beamed with love. He looked into Laura's eyes. "Then if Laura will have me, we'll be married and the contract will read Laura Roberts and Starlight. Is that acceptable to you, Laura?"

"Yes." Laura barely breathed the answer before Guy dipped his head and kissed her. Her heart flipped, sending a thrill through her. A thrill more intense than any she'd felt while performing one of her daring tricks. It was a feeling she planned to experience the rest of her life. With Guy.

* * * * *

REQUEST YOUR FREE BOOKS!

2 FREE INSPIRATIONAL NOVELS
PLUS 2
FREE
MYSTERY GIFTS

Love Inspired

YES! Please send me 2 FREE Love Inspired® novels and my 2 FREE mystery gifts (gifts are worth about $10). After receiving them, if I don't wish to receive any more books, I can return the shipping statement marked "cancel." If I don't cancel, I will receive 6 brand-new novels every month and be billed just $4.49 per book in the U.S. or $4.99 per book in Canada. That's a savings of at least 22% off the cover price. It's quite a bargain! Shipping and handling is just 50¢ per book in the U.S. and 75¢ per book in Canada.* I understand that accepting the 2 free books and gifts places me under no obligation to buy anything. I can always return a shipment and cancel at any time. Even if I never buy another book, the two free books and gifts are mine to keep forever.

105/305 IDN FVYV

Name _____ (PLEASE PRINT)

Address _____ Apt. #

City _____ State/Prov. _____ Zip/Postal Code

Signature (if under 18, a parent or guardian must sign)

Mail to the **Harlequin® Reader Service:**
IN U.S.A.: P.O. Box 1867, Buffalo, NY 14240-1867
IN CANADA: P.O. Box 609, Fort Erie, Ontario L2A 5X3

**Are you a subscriber to Love Inspired books
and want to receive the larger-print edition?
Call 1-800-873-8635 or visit www.ReaderService.com.**

LIDIR13

REQUEST YOUR FREE BOOKS!

2 FREE INSPIRATIONAL NOVELS
PLUS 2
FREE
MYSTERY GIFTS

Love Inspired

HISTORICAL
INSPIRATIONAL HISTORICAL ROMANCE

YES! Please send me 2 FREE Love Inspired® Historical novels and my 2 FREE mystery gifts (gifts are worth about $10). After receiving them, if I don't wish to receive any more books, I can return the shipping statement marked "cancel." If I don't cancel, I will receive 4 brand-new novels every month and be billed just $4.74 per book in the U.S. or $5.24 per book in Canada. That's a savings of at least 21% off the cover price. It's quite a bargain! Shipping and handling is just 50¢ per book in the U.S. and 75¢ per book in Canada.* I understand that accepting the 2 free books and gifts places me under no obligation to buy anything. I can always return a shipment and cancel at any time. Even if I never buy another book, the two free books and gifts are mine to keep forever.

102/302 IDN F5CY

Name	(PLEASE PRINT)
Address	Apt. #
City	State/Prov.	Zip/Postal Code

Signature (if under 18, a parent or guardian must sign)

Mail to the Harlequin® Reader Service:
IN U.S.A.: P.O. Box 1867, Buffalo, NY 14240-1867
IN CANADA: P.O. Box 609, Fort Erie, Ontario L2A 5X3

Want to try two free books from another series?
Call 1-800-873-8635 or visit www.ReaderService.com.

* Terms and prices subject to change without notice. Prices do not include applicable taxes. Sales tax applicable in N.Y. Canadian residents will be charged applicable taxes. Offer not valid in Quebec. This offer is limited to one order per household. Not valid for current subscribers to Love Inspired Historical books. All orders subject to credit approval. Credit or debit balances in a customer's account(s) may be offset by any other outstanding balance owed by or to the customer. Please allow 4 to 6 weeks for delivery. Offer available while quantities last.

Your Privacy—The Harlequin® Reader Service is committed to protecting your privacy. Our Privacy Policy is available online at www.ReaderService.com or upon request from the Harlequin Reader Service.

We make a portion of our mailing list available to reputable third parties that offer products we believe may interest you. If you prefer that we not exchange your name with third parties, or if you wish to clarify or modify your communication preferences, please visit us at www.ReaderService.com/consumerschoice or write to us at Harlequin Reader Service Preference Service, P.O. Box 9062, Buffalo, NY 14269. Include your complete name and address.

LIHDIR13R

ReaderService.com

Manage your account online!
- Review your order history
- Manage your payments
- Update your address

> ### *We've designed the Harlequin® Reader Service website just for you.*

Enjoy all the features!
- Reader excerpts from any series
- Respond to mailings and special monthly offers
- Discover new series available to you
- Browse the Bonus Bucks catalog
- Share your feedback

Visit us at:
ReaderService.com